Angel on His Shoulder

Revised Edition

CHARLES RAY

Uhuru Press
North Potomac, MD

This book is a work of fiction. Names, descriptions, places, and incidents are products of the author's imagination, or are used fictionally. Any resemblance to actual events or persons, living or dead, is purely coincidental.

For information about this and other works of this author, contact the author at charlesray.author@gmail.com.

Angel on His Shoulder, first published June 9, 2010, CreateSpace Independent Publishing Platform.
IBSN: 1453647805
IBSN-13: 978-1453647806

Printed in the United States of America.

Charles Ray

NOTES ON THE REVISED EDITION

Angel on His Shoulder is a story that sprang from a 'what-if' exercise I like to play. I started writing it, stopped, and then picked it back up again. When I finally published it, way back when, I was relatively satisfied with it – but, being new to the world of self-publishing, I did a lousy job of layout and cover design.

Well, here it is 2015, and I now know a lot more about layout, formatting, and cover design, and what's more, I know a lot more about where I wanted this story to go. So, I pulled up the old manuscript, started on page one, and after a lot of weeding and pruning, I offer readers a revised – and hopefully, much better – edition.

The old cover was uninspiring . . . hell, might as well be honest - it was as boring as watching paint dry. I think the new one better portrays the book's content. I've stayed true to the original. Winston Nesbitt is still a loser, and his grandmother is as impish and salty as ever. But, I do believe it's a better story.

Authors only thrive when their books are read, and reviews help attract readers. If you liked this book, do please leave a review on Amazon or Goodreads. If you're a book review blogger, a snippet on your blog would be much appreciated. If you have any comments, you can reach me at charlesray.author@gmail.com.

Charles Ray

"He who is older than you by one night, surpasses you by one idea." - **Arab proverb**

Chapter 1
■■

Winston Nesbitt's grandmother died when he was twenty-four, and on his fortieth birthday she came back.

She had tried to come back earlier, a week earlier in fact, but her inexperience at being a spirit from beyond the realm of the living, combined with Winston's lack of imagination, had made it difficult. Actually, it had just made it impossible. She couldn't figure out how to get him to notice her. He wasn't the type to notice anything out of the ordinary.

Winston was one of those ordinary people, ordinary to the point of boring. If it didn't fit his normal frame of reference, he couldn't see it, think of it, or believe it existed.

One morning she'd tried getting his attention by flipping the toilet lid closed as he was relieving himself. Instead of attributing it to a ghost or spirit – neither of which he believed in – he figured it was a stray gust of air from the ventilation system. In addition, he'd been so grossed out by the splash of amber liquid over his bare feet, he could think of nothing else as he took his second shower of the morning. A second time she'd rattled the curtains over the window of his bedroom, but he'd blamed that on the wind – he blamed a lot of things on the wind – and had tied the cords tight around them to keep them from flapping about.

She knew how much he loved to eat. Whenever he was upset, he ate. When he was happy, he ate. Winston was a bit on the pudgy side. In an effort to get his attention, she'd hidden in the refrigerator, waiting to say hello to him when he reached in for a snack or beer. That had been a disaster. Spirits aren't supposed to feel anything. Apparently, cold was the one exception. After an hour of sitting next to a six-pack of Heineken, her fingers had turned blue, and she was shivering so hard her clicking teeth sounded like a pair of maracas.

She'd just about given up when she decided to heck with it, she'd just pop into view right in front of his pudgy face and see how he handled it. What she actually thought was, "to hell with it, I'll just scare the piss out of him and see what happens." She would never say that to his face, though, because she knew Winston was a bit prissy about women using dirty language; Winston was prissy about a lot of things.

Now, having your grandmother, or anyone

else for that matter, come back from the beyond would be a traumatic experience for the hardiest of souls. Winston Nesbitt was, unfortunately, not the hardiest of souls.

He was in his bathroom at the time. It was 6:30 am, and he was shaving, getting ready to run out to the corner and catch the Number 74 bus to go to the Shady Grove Metro Station to catch the Red Line train and join the thousands of other bored commuters for the long trek to their boring offices in downtown Washington, DC. Preparing for another day just like all the other days, doing the same things he'd done the day before, and would do the following day. Now, just in case you think Winston was bothered by being bored, think again. He knew his work was boring, that in fact he was boring, but he was comfortable with that boredom. It was a predictable kind of boring, and Winston liked predictable. His definition of disaster was when things changed. Boring was good. Unpredictable was bad.

He'd just finished shaving the left side of his pudgy, brown face. He always shaved in exactly the same way; the left side first, then the right, and then the center, doing the space under his wide nose last of all. His routine never varied. Any change to his immutable routine would severely damage his tender psyche.

He was looking like a brown Santa Claus with half his beard missing. The white foam covered the right side of his face from the curve of his chin to his ears. His tightly curled hair, which he always had cut short, was also beginning to show speckles of gray at the temples, even at the tender age of forty. For reasons that had never been explained to him, all the men in his family turned gray early. He was happy, though, that he at least had a full head of hair, and was not beginning to go bald like a lot of the men his age that he knew. He kept his hair cut short so that all he had to do in the morning was brush it. But, even his hair brushing routine never varied. First he brushed the right side, starting with two downward strokes of the little triangle of sideburn, then straight back ten strokes. He then did the top – ten strokes. The right-side routine was repeated on the left side. Finally, he did ten strokes down the back. Not nine, never eleven, always ten.

Winston lived in a rather sumptuous brick colonial house; two stories with a finished basement that he hardly ever entered; five large bedrooms, each with its own full bath; only one of which he ever used; except for the bathroom downstairs off the sitting room, which he used on occasion. The house was in one of Maryland's wealthiest suburbs. Not the wealthiest; that was in nearby Potomac; but, a neighborhood just outside Potomac, in an unincorporated area that had once been farmland. The farmers, unable to keep up with property taxes, had sold to developers who built overpriced homes that were not quite as luxurious as the mansions in Potomac, but which cost slightly less than the million plus dollars those homes did. Winston's parents had bought the house twenty-five years previously, and sold the small brownstone they'd owned in the District of Columbia. They'd lived there from the time Winston's father had enrolled in the Howard University Medical School. They'd gotten a twenty year mortgage, which was paid off when Winston was thirty-five.

His grandmother had lived with them in the District, and had moved with them to Maryland. She had her own little apartment in the basement, which had been one of Winston's favorite places until he turned twenty. After she died, he never wanted to go back into the basement, and limited his trips to the absolutely necessary, like changing the filter in the furnace. There were just too many memories there for Winston to handle.

The house was in a community of similar houses, just off Dufief Mill Road. It sat just inside the ornate entrance which consisted of two large stone cairns that announced the name, *Potomac Vista.* The name was usually blocked by weeds which the Homeowners' Association could never seem to keep cut, despite the hundred dollar a month fee they assessed every homeowner in the community, and there was no 'vista' of the Potomac, which was three miles south of them. The association didn't take the same attitude toward owners, though. Let a lawn get a bit high and they were all over you;

He had a modest-sized back yard that had

once been enclosed by a six-foot-high white picket fence. His father had built the fence for privacy, but had taken it down after a dispute with the Homeowners' Association. Winston had never particularly liked the back yard, but he had liked the fence because it blocked the view from the neighboring houses, and gave him a place of solitude.

Winston didn't like doing yard work. Nor did he like paying the inflated prices to lawn services that hired South American laborers at less than minimum wage, pocketing the difference. He'd considered getting permission from the Homeowners' Association to rebuild the back yard fence so he could let the grass grow and their inspectors wouldn't be able to see it, but decided against it when he saw what a fence cost. So far he'd been lucky. The association hadn't noticed that he never mowed the back yard. Every Saturday during the growing season, he'd take the old lawn mower out of the garage and cut the postage stamp sized front lawn. It was a task that thoroughly tired him out. Just moving the heavy machine from the garage was strenuous, and at the end of the forty-five minutes it took him to do what one of the local teens could have done in ten if Winston had been willing to pay, he barely had the energy to move the mower back inside the garage.

Winston didn't own a car, because he didn't drive, so the mower had the garage to itself except for a few boxes his parents had left stacked against the wall. He'd never seen the need to get a driver's license. Fortunately, the state of Maryland issued a photo ID for those few people who had no desire to get on the Washington Beltway, endangering their lives and others, and this is what he used at the local Seven-Eleven on those few occasions when he had to cash a check in order to have ready cash during the week. The counter clerk at the Seven-Eleven, a skinny Indian from Mumbai who was darker than Winston, always looked askance at the strange man who had no car, but Winston took no notice. The man cashed his check, and that was all that mattered to Winston.

A person of unvarying routine, Winston was severely discomfited by anything that upset that routine. When the wind blew hard, his cable service would be disrupted; and, even if this only lasted for a few minutes, it was enough to send him into a fit of depression, causing him to nearly empty his refrigerator and pantry of anything edible.

He liked things to remain constant, because in constancy there was security.

As a consequence, the appearance of something that in the rational universe he inhabited was not supposed to exist constituted a major disruption of his routine.

He first saw her in the mirror. But, his eyes still bleary from having just awakened, he refused to believe what he'd just seen. One second there was nothing there, and then, there she was. She'd just 'popped' silently into view. Winston had a rapid internal debate with himself. How, he asked himself, does something *pop* silently? It's either silent, or it pops. It can't do both. But, it . . . she had, and that was curious. When he was able to focus clearly things got even more curious.

It . . . she . . . whatever it was looked just like Gran Gran, which was what he'd always called his grandmother, Sally Young. The same caramel colored complexion, high forehead and cheekbones, and the white-streaked hair pulled back in a serious bun. The same piercing gray eyes, that he remembered as a kid, regarding him with that same judgmental expression just before she'd say, "Winston, what's wrong with you boy? You can do so much better." She was always saying that to him, and he'd never understood what she'd meant by it. His life seemed to unfold as it was intended to unfold, so what was the problem?

The . . . his mind was still unable to attach a proper description to what he was seeing . . . had the same wiry frame and reed-thin arms, with rounded shoulders covered by a red and black plaid shawl over a gingham dress, which was what she usually wore. It was the way women dressed in the small Georgia town near Atlanta where she was born, and despite her decades of living in the DC area, she still preferred to dress like they did 'down home.'

The problem with the apparition, and his mind had sort of settled on that as an appropriate word, was that it was only about twelve inches tall. She'd been small, but never that small. Oh, and she was perched on his left shoulder.

He couldn't feel any weight, but there she was, all twelve inches of her, reflected in his mirror, sitting on his left shoulder swinging her right leg back and forth just as nonchalantly as you please. And she *had* popped into view. Not that he'd *heard* the pop, but he'd definitely felt it.

This, his mind finally told him, was impossible. Probably a result of something he'd eaten the night before. So, he closed his eyes and slowly counted to ten. But, when he opened his eyes, it . . . she was still there, looking at him with an impish grin on its . . . her face. He tried rubbing his eyes, but only succeeded in getting shaving cream in his eyes, which stung like the dickens. Rinsing helped the stinging, but the *thing* was still there staring back at him from the mirror.

Winston's brain tried stubbornly to deny what his eyes were seeing. There's no such thing as miniature whatevers that sit on your shoulder while you're shaving. That kind of thing only happens in B movies that play on cable late at night; the kind you watch when you can't get to sleep. Even in the movies, such things are hard to believe, so no way they could happen in real life.

Whatever this 'whatever' was, it was clearly a disruption in Winston's otherwise orderly if somewhat boring life. His stomach began to rumble as he kept staring into the mirror, and the apparition refused to fade away. It worried him. Not only was it a disruption in his routine, but it meant he was hallucinating, going crazy, or he was still asleep, and having the most realistic and disturbing dream of his life. It didn't matter to him which situation applied, for they were all disturbing. And, when he was disturbed he got hungry. When he got hungry, his stomach made this horrible noise that could be heard from quite a distance.

When he heard his stomach growl it upset him even more. He'd already eaten breakfast. He shouldn't be hungry while shaving. It wasn't part of his normal routine.

Then, he decided to do the one thing he'd so far not done. Instead of looking at it in the mirror, he turned his head slowly and looked directly at his shoulder. And, instantly regretted it.

Sitting there, mere inches from his half-lathered face, was the thing he'd seen in the mirror. Perched on, well, actually, floating about a half inch above his shoulder, now looking him dead in the eye, was a twelve-inch version of his grandmother.

"Good morning, Winston Lee," she said in that reedy voice he remembered so well. "It's been a while. Did you miss me?"

At that point, Winston Lee Nesbitt did what any red-blooded young man of 40 who lived alone, with an unvarying routine, who didn't deal too well with change, and who never did anything more exciting than watch the Fashion Channel late at night in hopes of catching a glimpse of a stray breast, would do when confronted by a foot-tall replica of his long dead grandmother speaking to him first thing in the morning as he was shaving.

He fainted.

Charles Ray

Chapter 2

When he came to, he was flat on his back on the cold tiles of the bathroom floor, still clutching his razor, looking up at the ceiling, and wondering how he'd wound up on his back on the cold tiles of the bathroom floor, clutching his razor, and looking up at the ceiling.

Then, he remembered, and he almost fainted again.

It was through no force of his will that he didn't faint. He didn't have the energy to faint. At that very moment, in fact, he had no energy or will to much beyond lie quietly on is back and wait to wake up, or be carted off to the loony bin; whichever was appropriate. If he was dreaming, he would really need to watch what he ate or drank before going to bed, because he didn't remember ever having a dream like this one before. If he wasn't dreaming, there would be a padded room full of people in white jackets who always walked softly and spoke in hushed tones who would watch what he ate or drank at all times, because, if he wasn't dreaming, he was crazy with a capital C.

As he lay there, he wished, really, really hard, that he was asleep, because, if this was a bad dream, it would be over when he woke up. But, he was beginning to suspect that it wasn't a dream, because he never had thoughts like this when he was dreaming.

Gran Gran, or the apparition that looked like a miniature version of her, had moved from his shoulder to a position on the tile floor – or about half an inch over the tile floor – about a foot to the left of where he lay. He could see her if he turned his head. He didn't want to turn his head, because he didn't want to see her, but he turned his head anyway, because he couldn't stop his head from turning. Like a motorist passing the scene of an accident who tries to tell himself he really doesn't want to see a mangled body hanging from a wrecked car, but who looks anyway, to see if there's a body in the smoking wreckage, he really, really couldn't help himself. She hovered there, hands on her bony hips, looking at him with that thinly disguised expression of impatience for which she was known from Pennsylvania to Florida. Winston and his cousins had all at one time or another had had that look bestowed upon them, and he felt guilty whenever it happened, even if he'd done nothing.

He felt guilty now, and he knew he'd done nothing.

"It's about time you woke up, Boy," she

said, making an impatient stamping motion with her right foot, which was funny since she was hovering and there was nothing for her to stamp her foot on but air. "I was beginning to fear your heart might have stopped. Can't have you passing away on me now, 'cause that just wouldn't be proper. 'Sides, I wouldn't know what to do if you up and died on me.

"Gr-, ga, gr-," Winston said. "Grack, gull, ga."

Winston did that a lot when he was confused. His tongue would get all cottony and refuse to respond properly to his mental commands, and he made sounds like a stuttering two-stroke engine from his mouth, and a deep gurgling from his ample midsection. At the moment he was as confused as he'd ever been in his life, and the sounds from both ends of his body were competing with each other.

"Quit chewing on your words, Boy. Talk like I taught you." She did that soundless foot stamp again. Winston had the presence of mind to notice that in addition to being able to hover, and stamp her feet with nothing to stamp them on, she cast no shadow. *Well of course,* he thought, *whatever this is, it can't really exist, and things that don't exist wouldn't cast shadows or make sounds, now would they?*

"Boy, you do think the strangest things," the apparition said.

Just what that meant, Winston in his present state of mind was not sure. What he was sure of was that he wanted what was happening not to be happening. It wasn't supposed to be happening in the first place, and the sooner it stopped happening, the better he'd feel.

Frankly, Winston wasn't sure which bothered him more; the twelve-inch version of his dear departed grandmother hovering soundlessly over the tile floor just inches from his face; or, just the fact that, except for her reedy voice, she made no other sounds. Not one. Not a 'whoosh,' not a 'swish,' nothing. Even when he was barefoot, he made 'swooshing' sounds when he walked across the bathroom floor; he even made little whispering sounds when he walked on the carpet in the bedroom. It just wasn't natural to make no sound when you moved about. It was even more unnatural to be able to float about like a dandelion spore on a windless day. People don't float around like that.

But then, he remembered; this wasn't a people . . . person . . . whatever. Despite an uncanny resemblance to his grandmother, down to her reedy voice, it just couldn't be a person, and it couldn't be his grandmother. His grandmother had died. He knew that because he'd attended the funeral. He was reasonably sure that people didn't come in such small sizes with the ability float in the air, at least not in the real world of sane people. Maybe things like that happened in the world in of crazy people. He couldn't be sure, having always, until this very moment, thought of himself as sane. He'd never even had a conversation with an insane person, at least, not to his knowledge. He wasn't even sure one *could* have a proper conversation with an insane person. The only crazy people he'd ever seen briefly – and peeking briefly was all he'd ever done, because Winston Nesbitt would never be so rude as to stare – had been the homeless on the streets of Washington, DC after President Reagan had cut off the funding for the looney bins, forcing them to release almost all of their inmates to the streets. The ones he'd briefly seen seemed to always be talking to unseen companions, and didn't seem to have much time for the sane passersby, except to occasionally ask for money.

Winston tried to reassure himself that what he was seeing was just some kind of illusion brought on by eating too much fat and drinking too much beer too late at night. *Just have to change my eating habits, that's all.* Yes, he thought, that has to be it. He'd read somewhere that eating just before going to bed could cause all sorts of problems. He didn't recall if hallucinations had been one of the problems listed, but reckoned they must have been, because he was definitely having a hallucination.

Then, Winston's mind being, well, Winston's mind, he wondered why his grandmother would be appearing before him in any size. She'd been dead for years. It couldn't be that she'd come back to haunt him. He'd been her favorite grandchild, and except for a few incidents had never done anything to *really* upset her. There'd been that one time when she came into his bedroom unannounced, an incident he blushed when he remembered, but she hadn't seemed all that upset at the time. She'd seemed to be more amused in fact.

Winston didn't care much for funerals, but the dutiful grandson he was, he'd gone along with all the other relatives, and it turned out that he was the only member of his family to break down and cry when they began lowering the coffin into the ground. His mother, a very sensitive person, had merely sniffled, and his father, who never cried or showed weakness, stood stone-faced and silent, staring off into the distance. The rest of the relatives stood around in clusters, depending upon which region they'd come from, some of them sniffling, and some, like his father, stone-faced. Winston, though, broke down and blubbered like a baby.

He threw his chubby frame down onto the green felt carpeting framing his grandmother's grave, clutching at the coffin, whimpering, mewling, yowling, and making a right and proper spectacle of himself.

Except for his mother and father, who he was sure just wanted to forget the whole thing, the family talked about his performance every time they got together, which mercifully, was only once every two to three years. Winston had never really liked attending family functions, and after five years, stopped going altogether.

They never said anything, but his parents seemed secretly relieved. Not that it mattered. He figured his graveside performance would be forgotten soon enough, and when it did, no one would notice he was no longer in attendance at family functions, since they never talked *to*, only about him.

Winston rolled over and slowly pushed himself up into a sitting position. He rubbed his eyes and shook his head, sending flecks of foamy lather flying all around, making little mounds on the tile floor and little blobs that clung to the walls.

The apparition ducked a glob of foam that sailed over its head and splashed against the wall, where it began to slowly ooze down toward the floor.

"Watch it, Winston Lee. That stuff stings if it gets in your eyes." That was something he'd already discovered. "And," she continued. "You're not going crazy. At least, you're no crazier than anyone else in this town. I do declare, Boy, you have the strangest things rattling around in that head of yours."

Winston shook his head, slowly this time to avoid flinging foam. If this was a ghost, it was a remarkably well informed ghost. Only his grandmother had used his first and middle names when addressing him, a relic of her Deep South upbringing.

"I'm sorry," he said. "I didn't mean to . . ." He stopped, as he realized he was engaged in a conversation with something that couldn't possibly exist. "It must be the chili and beer I had last night," he muttered. "Definitely shouldn't have had that third beer."

"What in blazes are you talking about, child?"

Winston looked like he was on the verge of crying.

"This can't be happening," he said.

"What can't be happening," she asked.

"I'm seeing things. That's it, I'm seeing things. Or, maybe I'm still asleep and this is all a bad dream. Any minute now I'll wake up in my bed and have to get up and get ready for work."

The problem with that theory was that the damp tile floor felt awfully real, and his fleshy buttocks were beginning to ache from the cold. And, he had a pain in the back of his head from where it had struck the tile when he fell.

Processing what was happening to him was difficult. This was the kind of thing that only happened in boring old movies. This was the twenty-first century, and such things didn't happen in this day and age. There had to be a logical, scientific explanation for what was happening, but try as he might, he could come up with nothing.

Slowly, ever so slowly, he levered himself upright. He stood, holding onto the edge of the sink, looking down at the apparition, which was now slowly rising up to his eye level. No matter how hard he willed it, it just wouldn't disappear. *Darn it, maybe it's not the beer.*

Maybe I suffered a concussion when I fell. That, of course, didn't explain how he'd seen it before he fell.

"Winston Lee Nesbitt, you stop being such a foolish child right now," the thing in front of him said. "I'm your Gran Gran. Don't you recognize me? Don't you go telling me you forgot what I look like." She floated closer to his face.

"But, you, er, I mean, my grandmother died sixteen years ago," he said directly to the apparition for the first time.

"Well, of course I did," she said. "I was at my funeral, remember? You really cut up, you know. Crying all over my coffin like that. Anyway, I'm a . . . spirit now."

"B-but, that would mean you're a ghost, and there's no such thing as ghosts."

"Is too such a thing," she said. "Of course, we prefer to be called spirits. Sounds a lot more fitting and sophisticated, don't you think. Ghosts are bad things, while most people think spirits are good . . . well, mostly good anyway. As a reward for living a good life, I became a spirit, so don't you be calling me a ghost, you hear."

"Okay, you're a spirit, then. Doesn't matter, because there's no such thing as spirits either, except for the kind you find in a bottle, and I don't indulge that kind."

"Boy, you don't know what you're talking about," she countered. "Spirits do exist. I know, because I am one. And. I'm here as you can plainly see, you silly ninny."

"So, you're a gho-, er, spirit. Why are you here in my bathroom at," he looked at his watch. "Twenty after six in the morning, scaring the bejeezus out of me while I'm trying to shave and get ready for work."

She smiled at him, that angelic smile he remembered from his childhood when she would pull him up on her bony knees and tell him what a good little boy he'd been, just before giving him a piece of his favorite candy, the long black licorice that used to stain his tongue and gross his mother out to no end. He still liked the occasional piece of licorice.

"Now, we're getting somewhere," she said. "I'm here, Winston Lee, because you're forty years old and you haven't done anything with your life. I'm here to give you guidance and put you on the right path, and I'm not leaving until I do that. Spirits don't just flit around doing nothing. Everything has a purpose, and the purpose of most spirits is to help. And, believe me, Boy, you need that help more than most people."

Oh great, I'm having a hallucination, and it wants to manage my life. That, at least, was consistent with the experience of his first forty years. Someone else was always managing him. He'd thought when his parents moved away and left him alone in the house, that part of his life was over, but his bosses at work managed his work life so much the absence of his parents had made no difference.

"And, just how do you plan to do that," he

asked. "I mean, didn't you give me enough guidance and help when you were alive?"

"I haven't figured that part out yet. Apparently, I didn't finish what I should have done when I was alive, so I have to find out what I missed doing, and do it. I don't have a lot of practice at this, though. I'm new at being a spirit."

"But . . . what have you being doing for sixteen years?"

"Uh, time doesn't work in the spirit world the same as it does out here. One minute I'm in a hospital hooked up to a lot of tubes and things, and my heart stopped beating, and the next thing, I'm . . . well, here I am. I know a lot of time has passed, because you look a lot older than I remember, but it doesn't feel like all that much time has passed. I can still smell that hospital. Anyway, I've got this unfinished business. Sounds like fun, doesn't it?"

Yeah, fun. Like going to the dentist is fun. Like getting a colonoscopy is fun. Winston didn't like fun. Whenever people were having fun around him, they had *all* the fun. All he ever seemed to get out of it was misery.

The longer he talked to the apparition, though, the easier it became to except it's existence, and except that it was his grandmother. He'd spent his entire life doing what other people told him to do, so this wasn't really that much of a change. If this spirit, his grandmother, was determined to take over his life, there was probably nothing he could do about it.

"Okay, Gran Gran. But could you please go somewhere else so I can finish shaving and showering?"

"Aw, Winston Lee, sweetie, I've already seen everything you have. You forget . . . I used to bathe you." She cackled. "You can be such a prude sometimes."

If Winston's face had been a lighter brown, it would have turned red. As it was, he turned a darker brown, his face wrinkled up, and his eyes watered. He looked as if he wanted to cry.

"I am not a prude. I just think there are some things that should be done in private, so do you mind?"

She laughed. "Still the same Winston Lee. You didn't even like me undressing you when you were a baby."

And then, she disappeared. Just like that. One second she was floating there in front of his face talking to him, and the next, there was only empty air.

"Hi-ho, Hi-ho, it's off to work we go." – **Dwarves and commuters**

Chapter 3

Thanks to his grandmother's untimely visit, and the time he needed to rub ointment on his aching head and comb his hair again, Winston didn't have time to fix breakfast, so he planned to stop and grab a bagel and coffee at the Korean deli near his office. It wasn't the best of breakfasts, or his preferred breakfast, but under the circumstances it would have to do.

His boss was always a problem if he was even a minute late for work. Heck, his boss gave him trouble even when he was, on rare occasions, early for work, or, as was usual, he was on time. After the conversation with his grandmother – and, he was now fully accepting that this was, in fact, his grandmother's spirit – he decided that he would try as hard as he could to avoid trouble for the rest of the day.

He rushed out of the house at 7:15, barely

making it to the bus stop on time, and almost getting caught in the doors, as the driver closed them just as he was stepping on the last step. The bus was crowded, forcing him to stand in the aisle near the back, sandwiched between a large, very dark lady with bulky shopping bags in each hand, and a beefy white guy wearing paint-stained coveralls and smelling of turpentine and stale beer. The bus bumped and buckled, bouncing him against the two in turn, and causing him to sway like the pendulum of a grandfather clock. He couldn't decide which was worse, the smell of turpentine and stale beer when he bumped into the beefy guy, or the sharp pain in his hip when he collided with the large lady's shopping bag.

"Excuse me," she said when Winston said 'ouch' after the bag hit him for the fourth or fifth time. "Is my bag bothering you?"

"Oh, no Ma'am," he replied. "It's no problem. I just have a little pain in my back. I must have slept crooked last night."

She smiled at him, but didn't move the bag, and it kept bumping him, sending shooting pains up his back each time it did. He figured he must have hurt his back when he fainted. Just his luck – a sore head, a sore back, and a boss who'd probably be riding him all day long; oh yes, and having his grandmother's spirit dropping in unannounced. This was not going to be a normal day. The thought set his stomach to growling. The old lady looked askance at him, a disapproving frown on her dark face.

The beefy guy leaned into him, speaking past him to the lady, "I know what he means about sleeping crooked. Whenever I sleep on a wrinkle in the sheet, or get the wrong way in my bed, my back hurts me all day long."

"Me too," the old lady said, blowing the smell of garlic into Winston's face. "Of course, I just take a couple of aspirins and the pain goes away. And, you know, aspirin is good for your heart and rheumatism as well."

"Is that a fact? I guess I ought to try that. I have this ache in my knees sometimes. I wonder if that could be rheumatism."

"It could be," she said. "Then again, it could be arthritis. There's a lot of that going around these days, you know."

"Oh yeah," the beefy guy said. "My mother has real bad trouble with arthritis."

"I know how she feels." The woman shook her head. "Sometimes my arthritis hurts so bad I can't go up and down the stairs. You should tell your mama to try bathing with Epsom salt. When that old 'arthuritis' gets to bothering me, I just put a cup of salts in hot water and soak in it for a couple hours. Makes him go away for sure."

"Epsom salts? That's good for arthritis?"

"It sure to God is," she said, crossing her hand across her ample breasts. "I swear before God, that stuff is a miracle. They always talking on the television about them new medicines what cost an arm and a leg, but you just buy your mama a five dollar box of Epsom salts, and that arthritis pain will be gone."

"I believe I'll do just that. Goodness, this must be my lucky day. Imagine bumping into someone who could solve that problem for me. Ma'am, I don't know how to thank you."

"Shoot, no need to be thanking me. The Lord put us people on this earth to help each other. Now, if you have trouble with rheumatism, that's another matter. Epsom salts don't help too much with the rheumatism pains at all."

"Oh yeah? What do you use for that?"

"I eat a pinch of asafoetida every day," she said.

Winston corrected himself. It hadn't been garlic he'd smelled, but the pungent smell of the dried resin from the root of Ferula herb. His grandmother used the same stuff, which she got from a friend in Georgia. She kept it in a muslin bag she wore around her neck. The stuff smelled terrible.

"Asafoetida? What is it, and where can I get some," the man asked.

"You know anybody in Georgia or Alabama? They could get it for you." The old lady twisted around to reach into her purse, jamming her bag against Winston's spine. "I got some extra. Here, you can have this." She passed a noxious smelling brown wad wrapped in tissue across in front of Winston's face. The smell almost made him faint. "Just tell her to eat a pea-size bit every morning soon's she gets up."

"Thank you, I'll do that."

It went on like that for the rest of the ride, the longest 45 minutes of Winston's life; the two of them discussing various ailments across Winston as if he wasn't even there. Between the pain from her bag jammed into his back and the noxious fumes coming from the man's mouth – and, he'd turned now to face the woman so that every time he spoke a foul odor seemed to scrape across Winston's face, he was on the verge of throwing up. Since he'd had to skip breakfast, though, there was nothing in his stomach to come up, which only made him even more uncomfortable, and caused his stomach to rumble even louder. Each time it did the woman would shoot him a disapproving look. The happiest moment of his life was when the bus pulled into its bay outside the Shady Grove Metro Station.

Inside the station, he had to buy a ticket for the turnstile, but the machine rejected the first two bills he tried to insert in the slot, making an annoying beeping sound as it spit them back at him. He fumed and uttered *dang* and *drat* under his breath, fumbling in his wallet until he finally found a ten dollar bill that was smooth and unwrinkled, and that the machine accepted. He inserted the bill, watched it get sucked silently into the innards of the machine, and took the cardboard ticket that shot out of a slot on the right side of the machine. As he withdrew the card, the machine began spitting out his change in a loud clatter; all nickels and dimes. *Darn, with my luck, they'll rattle around in my pocket all day, then at the end of the day, they'll wear a hole in my trouser pocket and I'll lose them.*

He jogged to the turnstile and inserted the ticket into the slot, where it was promptly ejected. He tried again. Again it was spit out.

The station man, a burly black man with mid-length curly hair had watched Winston's losing battle with the ticket machine. He shook his head wearily as he walked to the entry turnstiles. He took the ticket from Winston's shaking hand, turned it around and inserted it. It zipped through the machine and popped up at the end, waiting to be retrieved.

"It helps if you put it in the right way," the man said. Winston would have sworn there was a sneer in his voice. "You ought to buy one of the new plastic SmartTrip cards. Then you wouldn't have that problem. You just press it against this little square and the gate opens. Just about everybody's using 'em now. Betcha pretty soon we won't even be selling paper tickets anymore."

Winston had seen the ads for the new cards, but he wasn't sure. He would have to pay five bucks for the card, and then remember to keep enough money for fares on it. That involved pressing it against a plate on the ticket machine, and he just didn't trust that it would work. He also worried about losing it. If he lost the paper ticket, he only lost the amount for one trip. If he had one of the new cards, he risked losing considerably more. He resolved to think about.

He bolted through the gate, snatching the ticket as he ran, and jamming it into his shirt pocket, all the while hoping he wouldn't sweat too much and ruin it. He jogged up the escalator, careful not to bump anyone as he did, and made it onto the train just as the doors were closing. He breathed a sigh of relief that the doors hadn't made contact with his body. That would have earned him the enmity of his fellow passengers, because that meant the doors couldn't close properly, and sometimes when that happened, the drivers made everyone get off the train and took it out of service. That meant waiting for the next train, which was guaranteed to be packed to capacity, making for a ride that was more uncomfortable than usual.

The fact that he hadn't caused such a catastrophe didn't keep the other passengers from glaring at him. The looks seemed to be saying, you dolt, you almost interfered with our commute.

Winston tried his best to ignore the glares. He plopped into an inward facing seat near the center door, next to a skinny, brown-skinned girl wearing a green wool sweater and a gray scarf that left just the front of her elfin face visible. From the scarf, Winston guessed that she was Muslim, so he was careful to avoid touching her. She shrank against the plastic panel, and stared down at the floor. The doors slid back open, closed, and then they opened again. "This is the Red Line Train to Glenmont," the driver's raspy voice announced. "Next stop Rockville. Good morning and welcome aboard. Thank you for riding Metrorail."

"Bing-bong, Bing-bong. Step back, the doors are closing." The mechanical voice of a woman who sounded like his old high school librarian, all stern, cold, and unforgiving, came from the speakers. *"Bing, Bing, Bing! Step back and allow the doors to close!"* By now, the doors were already closed, so the harsh tone, in Winston's view, was unnecessary.

The train lurched into motion, causing Winston to brush against the girl, who shrank even more against the plastic panel. Even after the train settled in at its normal speed, the car still swayed a little. Across from him, he watched with fascination as a woman applied eye shadow, wondering how she managed to keep from spearing herself in the eye. He found this habit rude. Putting on makeup was one of the things he felt should be reserved for the privacy of the bathroom or bedroom, but at least she wasn't doing what he'd seen one man do – use a cotton swab to clean out his ears, inspecting the greenish-brown gunk on the end each time he pulled it from deep inside his ear.

As much as people doing their morning toilette bothered him, it paled in comparison to how he felt about people who completely ignored the rules about eating and drinking on the train. He really hated when someone got on with a greasy paper bag containing a bagel and cream cheese, or a burger and fries, and they sat next to him. Worse yet, was those who got on with their plastic mugs filled with steaming hot coffee. Often, they'd be looking directly at the "No Eating or Drinking' signs as they ate or drank. The food always smelled like rancid grease, and a drop or two of the coffee was sure to be spilled on his pants or coat sleeve.

After finishing their meals, most people just crumpled up the containers and left them on the seat, another violation of the rules.

That was what bothered Winston. Not following the rules. That's what rules were for; to be followed. He always followed the rules.

Winston sat back and sighed. He wasn't looking forward to the day ahead. It was already off to a bad start, and appeared to be slanted in a downhill direction. Once he got to the office, he knew, it would get worse.

He had a couple of reports that were overdue, and Leland Carter, his boss, would start bugging him about them, delaying his work and making them even more overdue.

At least he had the quiet time of the subway ride, at least as quiet as one might expect from a conveyance that creaked, squeaked, groaned, and lectured you in a stern librarian's voice at each station.

"You know, I don't remember the Metro being so crowded before," his grandmother said.

The statement struck Winston as funny. He chuckled. He only remembered his grandmother riding the subway once, and she'd complained about the crowds and insisted afterwards that his father drive her everywhere she had to go. *Must be absent-minded.*

"I am not absent minded," she said, and popped into view directly in front of his face.

Winston bolted upright, pressing his body against the car's wall. The girl next to him stared at him in horror. Several heads turned his way.

Oh, my goodness, she's back.

She floated toward him and perched on his left shoulder, only inches from the now frightened girl.

"What are you doing here? And, by the way, I wish you'd stop doing that," Winston said in a hushed tone.

"I'm on m-my way to school, and I d-didn't do anything," the frightened, quivering girl said. She looked as if she was about to try and claw through the plastic.

"Oh no, not you . . . I was talking to . . . oh, never mind," Winston said, waving his right hand at her. "Sorry, I was just, I mean, oh never mind. I was just thinking out loud."

He hunched in the seat, wishing he could become invisible. *Now is not the time for this.*

"*Of course it is.*" A voice inside his head said. "*You just have to relax and think what you want me to know. You never did learn to relax.*"

"*What the . . . now I'm hearing voices? I must be going crazy after all.*"

"*No,*" his grandmother's voice said. "*You're not going crazy. You're hearing me, so that makes it a voice, not voices. That's one of the advantages of being a spirit. We don't have to talk out loud. Comes in real handy when you're in a crowded place, and you want to have a private conversation."*

"You mean I just think what I want to say, and you can hear me?

"I don't know if you can say I hear you. Let's just say I know what you want me to know."

Winston thought about it for all of ten seconds.

"Okay, Gran Gran, I think I get it. But, tell me . . . why aren't the other passengers reacting to a little person sitting on my shoulder?"

"That's easy. They can't see me or hear me. We spirits are only visible to those people that have the special spirit vision, or those close to us. Guess there are no special people here, so only you can see and hear me."

"That's pretty neat. You can hear when I think at you. Hey, wait a minute. You can hear what I'm thinking. That means you can read my mind."

"Well, in a manner of speaking, I guess you could say that."

"Good grief. That means I have no privacy at all."

"Hon, if you think you have any privacy left in this country, you haven't been paying attention. This Internet thing and all the telemarketers long ago broke down any walls of privacy you had left. That is, the ones the

government didn't already take down years ago."

"B-but, I at least had the privacy of my thoughts. With you able to know what I'm thinking . . . well, it's just too much."

"Winston Lee, you quit being such a cry baby. Okay, okay, if it'll make you feel any better, I won't look too close at what you're thinking. Hell fire, Boy, most of it's boring anyway. Lordy, I never in my life saw anybody like you. Don't you ever think about anything interesting?"

Winston wasn't paying much attention. He was trying to shut his mind down. Boring, indeed. He had interesting thoughts. He just wanted to keep them to himself.

"Not really," his grandmother thought. *"Okay, okay, I know I promised. I won't listen to anything else unless you're thinking directly at me. I won't listen to any of your other thoughts. Good Lord, Boy, you sure are fussy."*

Winston didn't notice that she crossed her fingers behind her back.

"Thank you," he thought.

Chapter 4

It would have been nice if the rest of the ride had gone smoothly. Winston was so wrapped up in his mental conversation with his grandmother, though, that he completely forgot about the rest of the passengers jammed into the overheated subway car with him.

Winston was the type of person who could not *not* react to something said to him, or in this case, thought at him. He was unfortunately given to making faces in conversations, depending upon what was being talked about, and it turned out that the conversation inside his head was different than any he'd ever participated in before, so his face had gone through a number of contortions, which everyone in the car near him had seen.

By the time he arrived at the Gallery Place/Chinatown Station, the other passengers were convinced that he was some kind of crazy person who heard voices inside his head. That wasn't far from the truth – except for the crazy part.

"Gallery Place-Chinatown," the driver announced. "Doors opening on the right. Please take all your personal belongings and newspapers with you when you exit the train. Thank you for riding Metrorail and have a nice day."

Yeah right, Winston thought. Have a nice day – hah! As if the driver really cared. Winston had long ago come to the conclusion that most people didn't care about much other than themselves, and when they used phrases like 'have a nice day,' and 'how are you?,' they really didn't mean it. These were just empty utterances to fill the silence, or because they were expected in a given situation. When people asked how you were they didn't really want to know, nor did they care.

"*Bing-bong. Doors opening. Step back and allow customers to exit. When boarding, please move to the center of the car.*" The mechanical voice cut across the hum of the train. And, of course, as the passengers exited, half of the newspaper readers had left their papers in untidy piles on their seats or on the floor, and several people on the platform were trying to push their way in before everyone got off. Winston even noticed a number of Styrofoam coffee containers rolling around on the floor, some of them not completely empty if the shiny brown stains on the carpeting were anything to go by. The carpeting was already scruffy looking enough. It didn't need more help.

When Winston first got out of the Air Force and came back home to Washington, DC, he'd been impressed with the subway system. It was so much cleaner than the ones in New York and Chicago. The trains ran on time, and the transit police enforced all the rules. Over time, the police had gotten tired of being sued every time they wrote a citation for someone illegally eating or drinking on the Metro, so now they only enforced the 'No Smoking' rules, and in the wake of the 2001 terrorist attacks, spent their time running around in black uniforms looking like commandos. The trains were beginning to run late, or break down and not run at all, and he'd even begun to notice graffiti on some of the cars. As if that wasn't bad enough, the fares kept going up, and passengers were becoming as rude and short-tempered as people he'd encountered the few times he'd gone to New York City. In addition, with the increased number of former mental patients on the streets, you now had panhandlers and border line nuts riding the trains and mingling with the other passengers, which further exacerbated an already deteriorating situation.

As Winston exited the car, he noticed that the other passengers gave him a wide berth. He didn't begin to get jostled and pushed until he was on the platform where no one had seen his performance on the car. He was jostled and pushed along the platform, up the escalator, and out onto the street. This was usual, but now he had his grandmother perched on his shoulder, unseen by passersby, which was good, because she muttered and cursed loudly every time someone bumped into Winston.

"Dammit," she said. "Why are people so gosh darn rude. Winston Lee, you should push them back. What a bunch of horse's asses these people are."

Winston tried to pay her no attention. He kept his head down and made his way down the street.

"Why didn't you give those shitheads a shove back?" she asked angrily.

"That would be rude." He remembered to think at her rather than answering out loud.

"Now you're getting the hang of it." She smiled. *"Now we can talk anywhere we want and no one else will know. Of course, you really need to do something about the faces you make when you're thinking. Sort of spoils it if people think you're loony. Anyway, they're being rude, so it's only fair. Besides, you're bigger than most of them, so maybe if you pushed back, they wouldn't be so rude."*

"No, Gran Gran, I just can't do that." And, that was the end of the conversation as far as Winston was concerned.

He walked east on F Street, his grandmother chattering the entire way. He tried to ignore her, mostly successfully. If anyone had asked him later what was talked about, he'd have honestly been able to say he didn't remember. The profanity, as much as he hated it, stuck in his mind though. He hated dirty talk. Even when he'd been in the military he hadn't fallen into the habit of using dirty language. His avoidance of casual cursing had made him the butt of jokes in the barracks.

Even before the military, he'd had problems with language. In high school, he'd never joined in when the other students played the Dozens, a verbal game where insults (often having to do with female relatives) were tossed back and forth until someone lost their temper, which meant they lost the game. The really creative Dozens players could do it rapid fire and rhyming, and were admired by other students. Not Winston. He found the game disgusting and steadfastly refused to participate. This led to his being the target often, with insults like, "Winston is so fat, his mother has to use a wheelbarrow to roll him into the kitchen in the morning," or "Winston is a sissy who sits in a tree, pulling on his pecker, one, two, three. He rubbed so hard his dick got red, and Winston started crying and went to bed." These were two of the milder ones. It really got to Winston when they used the "F" word or the "N" word, which was often. His mother had taught him to never, ever use such language. He had taken her teaching on board to the point that he couldn't even *think* the two words.

His gauntlet run ended at the entrance of the Maxim Building, which was located on the corner adjacent to a shoe store.

Built at the turn of the century and never

renovated or updated, it reflected a bygone era when buildings were constructed in an elegant, ornate style to reflect the status of their owners and occupants. The Maxim Building's façade was marble, with deeply recessed windows on each floor, except the ground floor. As years passed, the once white marble had turned dirty gray. Set squarely in the center of the ground floor was the entrance. Oak framed double doors, each ten feet high and four feet wide, they had head-high stained glass insets decorated with gold filigree. The entrance lobby, which stretched halfway toward the back of the building, was a high-ceilinged space with marble walls and floors, and like the exterior, the white marble had turned light gray with age. The walls on right, left, and back were covered with a faded mural of a Revolutionary War scene of American colonists firing from behind hedge rows, fences and trees at orderly rows of red-coated British soldiers. Painted for the building's inauguration, the mural was cracked in places, with large patches of wall showing through in others. Lighting was from fixtures attached six feet up at regular intervals along the walls around the lobby. The fixtures resembled sconces of the late nineteenth century, with the light fixtures looking like large candles. Made of brass, they were rusted and corroded, shades of yellow, brown and green.

Near the back of the lobby, for about six feet in front of the bank of elevators, the floor was a dark ivory colored marble with white and beige swirls. When it rained and during winter, this part of the floor quickly became slick from wet shoes like an ice rink, causing people to slide rather than walk to the elevators. On more than one occasion, Winston had wound up sliding on his backside in front of the elevator just as the door opened, sliding all the way inside.

The elevators looked like they'd been installed when the building was first constructed. The doors were wood, and there was dark wood paneling inside, a ratty looking mahogany colored wood that was scratched and pitted from floor to ceiling. The control panel was a clunky array of buttons with the floor numbers etched into them. The numbers didn't light up, so you had to keep count as the elevator went up or down to know when you'd reached your floor. As it they moved from floor to floor, they creaked, squeaked, and swayed. An unnerving ride, no matter how many times Winston had done it.

The overall atmosphere of the lobby was that of the entrance to an asylum or prison. Even though Winston had never been in either, he was sure this is what they must look like. A stranger wandering in off the street, would take one look and immediately turn and leave, believing he'd either entered some super-secret government building, or a loony bin. The only thing about the Maxim Building that was secret was why anyone would want to be a tenant in the first place.

Consolidated Enterprises, the parent company of Advantage Consulting, the company for which Winston worked, owned the Maxim Building, which explained why Advantage Consulting was an occupant. CE's founder bought the building at a steal in the 1950s. After saving a ton of money on the purchase, and making a profit from the other tenants, he'd further enriched himself by foregoing any significant upkeep, other than what was absolutely necessary to pass the annual safety inspections. His son inherited the building in 1999, and, being his father's son, refused to make any effort to redecorate or modernize the building. Tenants were responsible for decorating their own spaces, and could do anything they wanted as long as the rent was paid on time. The Maxim Building was a lot like the troll that still thinks of itself as 'the prettiest bride at the wedding' when the rest of the wedding party is made up of fairies and sprites.

Winston made his way through the double doors, past the bored, frankly hostile looking security guard at the reception desk who looked wide-eyed at him at first, then frowned and barely glanced at his building pass. The double take caught Winston's eye. In all the years he'd worked in the building, it was the first time he'd noticed the security guard noticing his arrival in any way.

The elevator ride to the tenth floor was an ordeal, even more than usual. The car shuddered under the load of all the passengers who'd squeezed in with Winston, and Gran Gran ignored the two men, but insisted on critiquing the three young black women. One had hips that were too small, another's hips were too large, and the third had on too much makeup. They all wore skirts that were too short: "Showing all their business," she said. Winston's cheeks burned when she began assessing each of them as a potential marriage partner for him.

"That light-skinned one has nice wide hips. Bet she'd crank out babies faster than greased lightning," she said. She hovered near a beautiful dark-brown skinned woman who was about Winston's height. Her hair was done in a tasteful cornrow. "She's a bit too dark, but look at these titties of hers. She could suckle twins and have some left over. Hips are about the right size, too." She then flitted to the smaller one, beautiful despite having her head shaved. "Her ass is too small. Only a runt could squeeze out of her. And, despite the fact that her high yellow complexion combined with your brown might produce good looking babies, that shaved head is ugly. I'll bet you she's a lesbian."

Winston kept his eyes glued to the floor and tried to block his grandmother's running monologue, praying that his face wasn't giving away his sense of mortification at her graphic language.

He got off at his floor feeling fairly confident that he'd pulled it off, despite the fact that his face was burning with embarrassment.

When he arrived at his cubicle, the one in the farthest, darkest corner of the office, without a window or view, and with a ventilator shaft directly overhead that blew frigid air down on him all day long, Leland Carter was waiting for him.

The bureaucrat's bureaucrat, Leland Carter was also the owner of the Maxim Building. He always wore a dark, three-piece suit and his shoes were always polished to a high gloss. He was an inch shorter than Winston's five-eleven, and behind his back everyone in the company bet that he wore lifts to give him the height he did have. He was slight of build, much smaller than Winston, but had a little paunch like a melon that caused him to look like he was thrusting his pelvis forward in a dirty gesture. Whenever he noticed people looking at him, he sucked in his gut, sometimes until he was almost blue in the face.

Winston was unsure of Carter's age, guessing him to be in his mid- to late forties. He had no gray in his faded blond hair, but his hairline was crawling high on his skull, a condition he tried to conceal with a comb over that only succeeded in accenting it.

On this particular morning, he wasn't sucking in his gut, a clear indication that he was upset about something. Winston had a pretty good idea that he was the cause of Carter's upset, and was, therefore, in for a rough time.

"You're late, Nesbitt. It's Wednesday, not

Friday, not that it's acceptable to be late even on Friday," he said. He glared up at Winston, trying to look like the man in charge. Everyone knew that he *was* the man in charge, but sometimes Winston suspected that he doubted, which was why he was always such an ogre.

Carter stood with his hands laced over his crotch, his rounded shoulders back, his little melon tummy poking out, tapping his foot against the tile floor. He reached up and gently patted his comb over. "We had to reschedule the meeting because of you, you know," he continued. "Time is money, Nesbitt, and when people waste their time because of you, you're wasting the company's money. I hate to think how much was wasted by having three senior executives sitting around waiting for you."

Actually, Winston was only three minutes late, and he had no idea what meeting he'd held up. By his watch, and the clock on the wall of his cubicle, it was three minutes past eight. Considering the time it had taken him to walk from the elevator to his desk, he wasn't *actually* late. Winston guessed that Carter was up to his usual mind games. The man loved putting people on the defensive. Even though Winston knew this, it always worked on him. He shrank back in a defensive pose.

"Who is this little banty rooster, Winston Lee?" He'd momentarily forgotten his grandmother perched daintily on his shoulder.

"This is Leland Carter, Gran Gran. He's the owner of the company, and my boss." To

Carter he said, "It's just three minutes after eight, Mr. Carter. I'm not really late, since I came out of the elevator just at eight, and that's when the work day starts."

"You *are* late. If I say you're late, you're late." Carter's words were accompanied by a light spray of spit that spattered against Winston's blue tie. "I'd planned a strategy meeting for 7:30 this morning so we could go over your report on the Bradbury Corporation. And, the work day starts when I say it starts. Didn't you get my email?"

"What email?"

Carter snorted. "The one I sent at 5:45 yesterday."

"Oh, that email. The one that was sent fifteen minutes after I'd already left for home, and 45 minutes after the end of the official work day." Winston sighed. "But, you know I left the office at 5:30 yesterday. I stopped by your office and dropped off the McGruder Report. I didn't see the email about a meeting this morning."

"Well, Nesbitt, that's hardly my fault, now is it?" His voice really nettled Winston. "If you were more dedicated to work, you would have been here when I sent the email, and you'd have known about the meeting, and you wouldn't have missed it. Well, actually, knowing you, you'd have probably still been late, but you wouldn't have had such a lame excuse. Everyone else got the message and they were present and accounted for."

The everyone else he referred to were the

other executives, all of whom sucked up to Carter in order to stay in his good graces.

"What a lump of dog poop." While Winston didn't go in for such language, he couldn't disagree that his grandmother's description of Carter was how he felt about the man. *"Someone should scrape him up and dump in the nearest trash can."*

"That's for sure," Winston said.

"I'm glad you agree with me, Nesbitt," Carter said. "Let's hope it doesn't happen again. It wouldn't be good for your future with the company, you know." Carter seemed satisfied that he'd once again established his position in the pecking order. He smiled at Winston. "I've rescheduled the meeting for 8:30." He looked at his watch. "Just a few minutes from now, so get your stuff and meet me in my office. And, do try to make it on time, why don't you."

Without waiting for Winston to respond, he turned on his heels and strutted back to his office.

Gran Gran stuck out her tongue at him and made blew a raspberry, which caused Winston to choke back a giggle.

"Why do you let that little prick treat you that way, Winston?" She floated right in front of his face, looking sternly at him.

Winston shrugged and sighed. "He's my boss, Gran Gran. I don't really have a choice. If I argue with him I could lose my job," Winston said quietly.

He'd spoken quietly in the hope that no

one would hear, but he hadn't been quiet enough, and someone had heard. And, that someone caused Winston's already bad day to take a nose dive in the direction of worse.

"What did you say, Winston?"

Megan Berman, who occupied the cubicle next to Winston's, peered over the shoulder-high wall at him. A startled Winston took a step backwards. It would have been embarrassing for anyone else to have overheard him, but he didn't really care much what most of his co-workers thought. Megan, on the other hand, was another matter entirely. He cared very much what she thought.

"Uh, nothing, Megan," he said. "I was just mumbling to myself."

He was in a quandary, up the creek without a paddle, up a tree; he wanted to crawl into a deep, dark hole, or better yet, be back at his home in bed with the blanket pulled over his head. He would have given anything to be able to start this whole day over again.

Winston had a major crush on Megan Berman. He had, in fact, tried for over two years to work up the courage to ask her out, had even gotten close once or twice, but had always backed down at the last minute. He feared she'd turn him down, or worse, laugh in his face, and figured the best way to avoid rejection and embarrassment was not to ask in the first place. He loved talking to her, though, while he was at the same time, scared out of his wits whenever she was near, fearing that he'd say something stupid, causing her to laugh at him. He completely ignored the fact that he'd on many occasions said stupid things, and she'd not once laughed at him.

Megan was short, nearly a foot shorter than Winston. She had wide hips and slightly chunky thighs, and she always wore bulky blouses or sweaters that effectively concealed the rest of her body. They never managed to conceal the fact that her breasts were on the smallish side, when compared to her lower body. Her upper lip was thin, and her lower lip a bit thick, like she'd had a one-lip collagen injection. When she smiled, Winston could see that her two upper front teeth were a bit crooked and had a space between them that you could fit a pencil through, and she had something of an overbite. But, to Winston, she was the most beautiful woman on the planet.

Unlike Winston, who had lived with his parents until they up and moved to Florida, Megan had lived alone since graduating from George Mason University. Her parents lived in South Carolina, in a city whose name Winston could never remember any more than he could remember the name of the city in Florida where his parents resided. To him, anything south of Richmond, Virginia was just the Deep South, terra incognito.

Although, if he thought Megan wanted him to get to know the 'South' he'd consider it. She had a round face, with a smooth coffee and cream complexion, and the most beautiful brown eyes Winston had ever seen. And, she was one of the kindest people he'd ever met.

"You can do better, Winston Lee." His grandmother's thought interrupted his thoughts of Megan.

He'd forgotten she could 'hear' his thoughts. *Darn, have to . . . no, better not.*

"Better not what, Boy?"

"Nothing, Gran Gran. Just forget it, it wasn't important."

"Well, if you insist, I'll try. But, that girl seems to be just about the only thing rattling around in your brain right now. Don't tell me you're sweet on her?"

He wasn't about to tell her. He couldn't tell Megan how he felt, and he darn well wasn't going to tell anyone else. He especially wasn't going to tell his grandmother.

"Well, I'll be horn swoggled! Winston Lee Nesbitt, you are sweet on that girl. Now, Boy, you just get that kind of thinking out of your mind, and listen to your old grandmother. You can do a lot better. This woman is not the one for you."

"Gran Gran! Would you please stop it?"

The conversation with his grandmother, although it seemed an eternity to Winston, actually took place in a few seconds, but it was long enough for Megan to wonder if he wasn't a bit ill based on the panoply of expressions that crossed his face.

"I heard what Mr. Carter said to you," she said. "That was terrible. I think he deliberately waited until you were gone to send the email just so he could pick on you about missing the meeting. You know, no one else out here in the cubicles got the email he was talking about."

"It doesn't matter, Megan. If it makes him feel good to pick on me, it really doesn't matter." He shrugged. "I'd better get my report together. I'll talk to you later, okay?"

She shrugged and smiled at him. Then, she touched him gently on the arm, a slight caress, and then went back to her own work. He stood there looking dumbly after her, shivers coursing through his pudgy body.

Finally, he shook himself and squeezed into the tiny space that was his, and began rifling through the untidy stack of folders on his desk until he found the Bradbury Corporation file. He went over in his mind what he'd say during the meeting, which he anticipated would be more of an inquisition, leading him to have to completely redo all the work he'd spent a week doing. In the process of retrieving the folder from his desk, he caused the rest to tumble to the floor, scattering the contents all over. *Darn it. Now I'll have to lose more time sorting all that out.* In many ways, Winston's cubicle resembled his back yard. No matter how many times he tried to straighten it up, within an hour, it was a jumble again. After a few weeks of futile effort, he'd given up and learned to do the same thing he did with his back yard – ignore it.

Charles Ray

"What you don't know can hurt you, but it's better to avoid what you know can hurt you." - **Gran Gran**

Chapter 5

If a lottery was ever held for picking bad outcomes, Winston would win hands down. He could never guess when things would go well. Actually, things seldom went well for him – but, he always knew when things would go bad.

As he had anticipated, the 'Three Scourges' as he called them picked his briefing apart. They metaphorically ripped it into tiny confetti and tossed it in his face.

The 'Three Scourges' were the top management of Advantage Consulting, Inc.

Leland Carter, CEO and Director of Business Development, was Winston's direct supervisor, and the alpha male of the Scourges. He had the meanest eyes Winston had ever seen. Blue-gray, sort of icy, and he was always squinting as if a bright light was shining in his eyes, or as if he'd just sucked on a lemon. He made the drill sergeants Winston remembered from basic airman training seem like choir directors, and, unlike them, Carter never raised his voice. What he had done, though, was single Winston out for a special brand of cruelty, from the day he'd hired him seventeen years earlier, much in the way the leader of a dog pack will single out the runt of the pack. Hardly a day went by that Carter didn't do something to make Winston's day miserable.

Archibald DeMille was the chief operating officer. Winston wasn't sure what the COO did, because DeMille, who was the only other African-American in the company besides Winston and Megan, spent most of his time in his office with the door closed. Like Carter, he favored three piece suits. He also wore a hat whenever he was outdoors. He was bald except for a sprinkling of tightly curled hair at the temples and lower back of his skull. He wore round, gold-rimmed glasses, which made him look even older than he claimed to be, which was fifty. With his rotund frame, he looked like the Boss Tweed character in the cartoons. He seldom spoke to Winston, except to criticize. Winston figured he did this as a way of showing that he wouldn't favor him because of race, but he also noticed that no one else was on the receiving end of his barbs.

Scourge number three was John Park, a

second and a half generation Korean-American. The half generation part came from the fact that while his mother had been born in the U.S., his father had been brought to the country when he was three. Park was director of support, another job that Winston didn't understand, because he'd never received any support from him, nor had he seen him provide support to anyone else in the office. What Park did seem to be good at was joining the other two in tormenting Winston on a regular basis. And, to make it even more irritating, when he criticized Winston he'd lapse into the Korean habit of making a hissing sound or a rasping in the back of his throat. He also had a habit of making negative comments about people, especially people of color, which included the darker Asians like the Vietnamese or Cambodians.

Park didn't seem to like anyone, including his fellow executives. Winston had never seen him engage the other two in conversation. Carter and DeMille were always off in a corner deep in conversation, laughing and 'high-fiving,' while Park stayed in his office unless he had to come out to attend a meeting.

He had broad flat cheeks and almond-shaped eyes that combined to make him look sinister. His glossy black hair always had white flecks of dandruff that collected on the shoulders of his expensive suit jackets.

He was completely unlike the other Koreans Winston had met. The Korean lady who ran the deli down the street from the office, for instance, would occasionally say hello to him, and had once or twice tried to engage him in conversation. Winston, though, had been unable to understand her fractured English, so he'd simply smiled and nodded as she prattled on. Park, though, never smiled.

The three of them were waiting for him, seated at the small conference table in Carter's office. Carter sat at the head, with DeMille to his right and Park to his left. Winston sat at the foot of the table and pushed the Bradbury file toward his boss. Carter opened the manila folder and flipped quickly through the documents, far too quickly to have comprehended anything. He then slammed the folder shut and frowned down the table at Winston.

"Nesbitt, this report is totally unacceptable. You've missed all of the essential points, and have come to an erroneous conclusion. The client will be most unhappy if we submit this."

DeMille picked up the folder and glanced briefly at the first two pages of a fifteen page report with thirty pages of charts.

"Yes, I totally agree," he said. "What could you have been thinking when you wrote this?" He passed the file across to Park.

Park flipped through the report, at least glancing at each page. He even looked at the first two or three graphs before slamming it shut.

"S-s-s-s! Yes, I have-a seen-a the better

reports-u by the new worker," he said, and then made that irritating throat clearing sound.

For reasons Winston had never understood, Park, even though he'd been born in the U.S., and had graduated from Yale, he often insisted on speaking English like a newly arrived immigrant who'd studied English as a second language late in life. Winston didn't understand why the man did it, but whenever he did, he had to clench his jaws to keep from giggling.

"I don't understand," Winston said. "I read all the data carefully, and my conclusions are in line with the current trends. What exactly is wrong with the report? I'll do my best to try and correct the problems, if you'll just tell me specifically what's wrong."

Winston took a small pad from his pocket, put it on the table and took out his pen, holding it over the pad.

Carter inclined his head toward DeMille, who smiled broadly.

"Well to start with, Nesbitt," he said. "I have a real problem with this statement in the Executive Summary. You say that the client should consider divesting itself of subsidiary operations that are unrelated to the core business."

"Yes, Sir, one of the drains on Bradbury's budget currently is the cost of supporting operations for which they lack either expertise or a competitive advantage. If they divest themselves of these parts of the company, they will save . . . no, make money."

"We don't insult our clients, Nesbitt," the fat man said. "Their line of business is entirely their decision to make, and we must tread carefully when we touch on that subject. The temerity you demonstrate in assuming you know more about their business than they do is frightening. I'm sure there are sound business reasons for everything they do, and we are not about to question those reasons."

What a load of hogwash. Anyone with an ounce of common sense looking at their data would come to the same conclusion I did. What Winston had discovered was that Bradbury was squandering a third of its cash reserves and half its staff on activities unrelated to its core business, activities that had failed to ever turn a profit. He'd learned, though, that when the Three Scourges had made their minds up it was useless to argue points of logic. At such times it was prudent to just quietly go along. He made a note to redraft the sentence that DeMille objected to. It would mean, of course, that he'd have to go back through the entire report and check his charts and tables, ensuring that the numbers supported the new conclusion. He would rework the recommendations, but that basically meant junking the whole premise of the report, and tell them they were doing things right, which was an insult, because if they hadn't felt something was wrong, they wouldn't have asked for the analysis in the first place.

Before he could finish writing, Park thumped his index finger on the table. "You have-a the recommendation to client-u to consider 'just-u in time-u the deliver expendable office-u supplies and the outsource-u of the repair for office-u equipment-u."

It took Winston a few seconds to fully process what he'd said, and when he did, he wondered why Park was bringing it up. After all, one of the client's main complaints had been excessive overhead costs, and as far as Winston was concerned, this was an easy fix. "Yes, you see, they have a big problem with inventory costs and with recurring costs as well, especially the cost of office supplies and equipment. If they adopted just in time delivery and outsources a lot of their administrative work, it would save them a lot of money. They spend over $10,000 a month on photocopiers alone, and most of them are idle most of the time. If they had a pay-as-you-go copying contract, they'd spend about $500 a month, depending on the amount they do, and they'd free up the space currently occupied by copy machines and supplies for more productive use."

"But, we never tell the client to get rid of the things," Park said in an insistent tone, still mangling the end of most words.

This, Winston knew, was incorrect. They often recommended outsourcing and divestment as ways to save money, and their clients appreciated it, because it allowed them to lay the blame on the consultant when the inevitable complaints came in from employees affected by such downsizing activities. He made a note of Park's comment nonetheless.

Carter had remained silent through this first part of the inquisition, but Winston knew he would not be outdone in the stupid comment department. He thumped the unopened folder that Park had pushed toward him.

"I have a problem with your section on information technology," he said. "You recommend Bradbury leverage new technologies and expand their IT staff. We want to save them money, and here you're suggesting they *spend* more. Can't you make up your mind?"

Winston was particularly proud of that section of the report. In it he showed how the company had lost money and competitive advantage by failing to employ some of the new technologies like email and video conferencing to cut down on overhead costs and improve employee efficiency. Like many older firms, Bradbury had relied on face-to-face meetings and written memos to convey data and instructions. By converting to electronic means, they could speed up operations, and involve more people at less cost and staff time.

"If they installed email and video conferencing, they could recover their cost in six months on employee travel alone, and over time, their expenses would be reduced by ten percent," he countered.

"I disagree," Carter said. "It seems like an unnecessary expense to me."

Coming from a man who often had to get

help from his secretary just to turn his computer on, and who frequently deleted documents accidentally, that should have been funny. But, Winston didn't feel like laughing. What he felt like doing was going to a dark corner to sit and cry. Carter knew as much about computers as Winston knew about piloting a space ship. Why he singled out that particular section for criticism was beyond comprehension.

The inquisition went on for over an hour, with the three executives taking turns throwing increasingly idiotic and contradictory comments at Winston, sometimes even contradicting their own previous complaints. The sole purpose of the exercise, as far as Winston could see, was to abuse and intimidate him. It probably made them feel important, he thought, and wanted to shout back at them. But, he needed the job, and being dismissed for insubordination wouldn't help him get another. Just the thought of being out of work and having to look for other work intimidated him.

"We need to make sure we encourage them in the direction of modernization and keeping up with the times," he said.

"They need to find-u ways to trim-u the overhead," Park said.

"In the dog eat dog world of business," DeMille added. "They have to learn to fish or cut bait. If they don't get into the race, they'll be left at the starting gate. Hell, they won't even get out of the stable."

What they meant by that, Winston had no idea. He finally agreed to redo the entire report.

"I want it on my desk by close of business," Carter said, ending the meeting.

Winston figured they'd satisfied themselves that he was sufficiently chastened for one morning, so, like a beaten dog, he went back to his cubicle, his tail between his legs. He had no idea *how* he was to redo it, or even if they expected him to make any changes. They'd made so many contradictory comments, he'd gotten lost and for the last twenty minutes of the session had done nothing but draw little curlicues in his note pad. All he could do was try his best to write a report that took their comments into consideration, and hope that it made sense.

Gran Gran had sat perched on his shoulder through the session, quiet for once, except for muttering under her breath whenever one of them said something really stupid.

When he got back to his cubicle, he threw the report on his desk, knocking over the coffee cup Megan had filled for him, and covering everything with the brown liquid. *Oh, well, why not! It's been such a lousy day, I might as well have to redo all the other reports as well.*

"It doesn't have to be so bad," Gran Gran said.

"Oh, yeah? And, just how is that?" Winston shot back at her, a whiny note in his thought. "I just work here. They're the ones in charge, and they never let me forget it. Gran Gran, I can't *afford to lose this job. At my age, jobs that pay a decent wage are hard to find."*

"You can stand up for yourself, Child. Be a man. You don't have to take that kind of treatment from anyone. Your father would never have stood for that. Why, he would have eaten that trio of jackasses for lunch, and then spit their bones on the floor."

"All resisting will do is get me fired. Besides, I'll never be like my father."

Through the cubicle wall he heard Megan's muffled voice, "Winston, you really need to stop talking to yourself. People are gonna start thinking you've lost it."

He hadn't realized he'd spoken aloud. "Sorry, Megan," he said. "So far, it's been a tough day."

And, the day wasn't even half over.

"I can imagine what you just went through. Is there anything I can do?" She stood and peered over the cubicle wall.

Actually, you can't begin to imagine what I just went through, because they'd never dare treat you like they do me. The Human Resources and EEO folks would have a field day if Megan, a woman *and* a minority, was verbally abused the way Winston was routinely abused. He, on the other hand, would have a hard time proving discrimination, given that DeMille was often one of his main tormentors. He'd learned to live with it. In fact, it didn't even bother him all that much anymore – just for a few minutes. But, with his grandmother hovering at his shoulder, he was afraid his routine was about to be upset. His stomach started making gurgling sounds.

"Thanks, Megan," he said. "But I don't think so. I'll just have to redo the Bradbury report. Mr. Carter wants it by close of business."

"That's a bummer," she said. "I guess that means you'll be working through lunch. Can I bring you anything?"

He hadn't thought about that. It would be just like Carter, though, to deliberately cause him to miss lunch.

"Gosh, that's awful nice of you."

"Anything special you want to eat today?"

"No," he said after a couple of seconds' thought. "Why don't you surprise me? You know me, I'll eat anything but the wrapper the food comes in." Once, he actually had been halfway through chewing up the paper wrap around his hamburger before noticing, but he didn't like to think about that.

"Okay," she said. "I'll get something really good."

Winston felt his heart pound. Anything Megan got for him would be really good. His cheeks felt flush.

"T-thanks."

He then turned his attention to the Bradbury report and his notes. His cramped handwriting was partially obscured by coffee stains, making it even harder than usual to read.

It was going to be a long morning.

Chapter 6

Winston spent the rest of the morning rewriting the report. He was careful not to put it in the pile with the other reports, which he had yet to collate.

His grandmother had disappeared somewhere, probably off doing whatever it is that spirits do, he thought. He could hardly have cared, as busy as he was trying to make sense of the executives' stupid comments. His dilemma was deciding which set of comments to focus on, given their contradictory nature. No matter what he did, though, he was bound to incur the wrath of at least one, probably two of them.

He shouldn't have cared, but he couldn't help but care. Advantage's top three executives were perverse examples of the validity of Murphy's Law in action. If something could go wrong, they'd find a way to make it go wrong, and blame Winston for it. They were Murphy's Law squared.

At a quarter of one, Megan came in carrying a bag containing, according to her, a super deluxe burger with fries and a large orange soda from the Burger King down the street from their building. The oil from the burger and fries had soaked through the paper bag leaving a shiny dark stain down both sides and on the bottom. His stomach did a double happy gurgle as the smell hit his nose. *Oh, I love you so much. I wish I could tell you that.* He grabbed the bag, mumbling his thanks, and promptly spilled a large splash of orange drink on the Bradbury report, which he'd just finished collating. *Dang, now I'll have to print and collate it again.*

He looked at the food. He smelled the food. And, then he looked at the ruined report. He decided that it would be wiser to put the food aside and finish the report, and then put it on top of his filing cabinet before touching the food again. Unfortunately, he forgot to wipe his fingers, so he promptly ruined the second copy, and had to do a third. He was sure he'd be getting a sarcastic note from the supply department after his third trip to the printer, but there was nothing he could do about it. He'd rather have supply on his back than Carter.

After finally getting the report done and safely out of range of his food, he wolfed down the burger, fries and drink, only spilling a little on the front of his shirt. At 3:30, he stood at the door to Leland Carter's office, the report in a plastic binder, held tightly against his chest. He knocked lightly and opened the door, but waited just outside. Carter didn't like people entering his office unless they were invited in.

Carter glanced up with a sneer, and then returned his attention to the trade magazine he'd been reading. He let Winston stand in the door for a full two minutes before looking up again. Slowly, he put the magazine on the edge of the desk, lining it up precisely, and then he looked at Winston.

"Well, don't just stand there, Nesbitt, come on in. What do you want?"

Winston walked tentatively into the office, stopping a foot from Carter's desk. "I've redone the Bradbury report like you wanted. I think I got all the comments incorporated, but some of them were a bit confusing, so I can't be sure."

Carter snatched the document from Winston. "I'll be the judge of whether or not they were confusing, or whether or not you did it right, which frankly, I doubt. Your original report was so poorly written, I wonder how even you understood it. I don't expect this to be what I want, but I do hope for the sake of your continued employment with this firm, that it's at least better than the original."

Carter was always making veiled threats.

Despite knowing that the threat to fire him was empty, Winston cringed. His lizard brain, that part of the organism that reacts in a 'fight or flight' manner to threats, only had a 'flight' mode. Fighting was not a part of his makeup.

Winston watched as Carter opened the binder, took a red marking pen from his shirt pocket, and, without even bothering to read it carefully, began scribbling all over it. He muttered as he marked, occasionally putting the pen to his lips, so he soon had little red spots all over his thin lips. Winston also noticed that there was a red blotch on his shirt pocket where the pen had leaked. *Bet his wife will give him an earful about that.* Then, he remembered, he didn't know for sure if Carter was even married. He didn't share personal information around the office, and had no family photos anywhere.

After five minutes, Carter slammed the folder shut, put the pen back in his pocket, and glared up at Winston.

"You missed all of the most important points, Nesbitt." He shoved the folder across the desk. "Do it again, and this time, try to get it right, will you. Good grief, man, you've been here long enough to do know how to do this in your sleep. Sometimes, I just don't understand you. You can turn in good work, but for some reason you turn in substandard trash. Don't you like working here?"

Without waiting for Winston to answer,

he picked the magazine up started flipping pages. Winston knew when he was being dismissed. Shoulders slumped; he picked up the folder and trudged back to his cubicle.

Back in his cubicle, sitting slumped in his chair, he opened the file. Sure enough, even though Carter's spidery scrawl was difficult to decipher, the changes he'd made meant that what he wanted was almost identical to the original draft of the report. Unfortunately, Winston had typed over the original without saving it, so he would have to retype the whole thing. Thankfully, he had an almost photographic memory, and the subject matter was something with which he was quite familiar. Bradbury would at least get a report that would be useful, provided they were willing to follow his recommendations.

He was thankful that he hadn't had his grandmother hovering over him while he worked, all the while no doubt she would have been telling him how foolish he'd been to take such treatment, and how he was squandering his talent and ought to stand up for himself.

Now, that, he thought wryly, would have it the perfectly terrible end to a perfectly terrible day.

"Fool me once, shame on you. Fool me twice, shame on you again." – **Winston Nesbitt**

Chapter 7

∎∎∎

Winston finished the report at 6:45, put it in a nice plastic binder, all neatly labeled, and left it in the folder attached to the wall just outside Leland Carter's office. Despite his having chided Winston for leaving 'early' the day before, Carter had disappeared a few minutes after 5:00.

There were few people left in the office at the late hour, just one or two of the other analysts who, like Winston, were working to meet rush deadlines. After all the years Winston had worked for the company, he hardly knew any of them by name, could never correctly connect the names with the faces of those he knew, and had spoken to none of them except to occasionally say good morning when he couldn't avoid them. Megan was the only other co-worker that he'd ever talked to at any length. Actually, she was the only other person in the office he'd really talked to at all. The one-sided conversations he had with the executives hardly counted.

Megan had departed shortly after five, and since he was in no mood to change the pattern of non-communication with the others, he quietly left without saying a word to anyone.

After leaving the building, he walked to the Metro station in growing darkness. Just as he stepped off the bottom of the escalator, his grandmother popped into view on his shoulder. He'd just about come to terms with her presence, so he didn't even blink when she appeared in the corner of his vision. She looked puzzled, but Winston decided not to ask her what was on her mind.

The Red Line train pulled into the station just as he arrived at the edge of the platform. He was pushed and shoved as passengers hurried off the train as soon as the doors slid open, and then pushed and shoved again by those waiting with him on the platform. Getting a seat was impossible, so he simply wedged himself against the plastic wall next to the door and tried to ignore the people whose bodies pressed against him.

"Dammit, Winston Lee," his grandmother's voice muttered in his head. *"Why do you let*

people push you around like this?"

Winston didn't feel like answering her, nor did he feel like being lectured to.

To keep her from pressing him on the subject of his lack of backbone, he decided to do something he'd learned as a kid, divert her by getting her to talk about herself.

"Where were you all afternoon?"

"Oh, you wouldn't understand." Her voice still sounded strange inside his head, although he was getting used to conducting these silent conversations. *"As a new spirit, I have to check in from time to time. I can't really describe to where it is I go or what I do, and it's not important anyway. How was the rest of your day?"*

Darn it, he thought, his ploy didn't work. She'd turned it right back on him. He gave her a quick and edited version of his day. It was boring. Out of the corner of his eye, he saw her yawning.

"Sorry, Gran Gran. I guess the kind of work I do is not very interesting to outsiders. Sometimes, it even bores me, but I'm used to it."

That was, unfortunately, the absolute truth. He did what he did, day in day out, year in year out, because it was what he'd been doing since leaving the Air Force, and he was unable to think of doing anything else. Without making any special effort, he'd become quite good at what he did – which consisted mainly of looking at numbers, making sense of them, and then making logical assumptions about them. It wasn't all that different than the work they'd taught him to do as a clerk in the Air Force. It just paid a tiny bit more, and he didn't have to wear a uniform.

He'd been doing it so long he no longer had to even think much about it. Worse, he wasn't even sure he was qualified to do anything else. Learning new skills would entail change, and most of all, he didn't want to change anything.

"It's not that it's boring, honey," she said. *"It's just that I've been sent . . . uh, I came back, to help you change your life, so you need to get used to change."*

"What kind of change?" Winston didn't at all like the sound of that.

"I'm not sure just yet. I'm kinda new at this, and I haven't quite figure out what I'm supposed to do."

If that was meant to make him feel better, it missed the mark. If indeed she'd come back to straighten out his life, it would have been much more reassuring if she had a plan.

As he was silently bemoaning her lack of a plan the train pulled into the Metro Center station, stopped, then suddenly lurched forward again. "Do not attempt to board this train. Train moving forward! Train moving forward!" The driver's voice over the speaker came at the same time as the forward lurch. Too late for the passengers who were standing and not hanging onto anything, or those getting up from the seats, the result was a jumble of bodies, elbows in backs, and general cursing and grumbling. Winston's body slammed against a tiny Asian woman standing next to him, knocking her against the wall. He muttered his apologies, but she waved them off. What he really wanted to do was shrink to his grandmother's size and become as invisible as she was.

The doors slid open with a wheezing sound. "Passengers on the platform, please allow passengers to exit the car before you attempt to board," the driver's voice said. "When you board, please move to the center of the car." At the same time, the librarian's voice came over the system, accompanied by chimes, *"Ding-dong! Doors opening. Step back and allow customers to exit. When boarding, please move to the center of the car."*

No one paid the slightest attention to either announcement. Passengers on the platform began pushing their way in as soon as the doors opened. More got off than got on, crowding the already crowded car even more, and everyone tried to get into or as close as possible to the spaces near the doors, which was where Winston was. As much as he would have liked moving to the center of the car, he was afraid he'd have to push people out of the way to do it, so he just shrank back against the car's wall as much as he could.

He found himself standing next to a tall, lanky blond with silver rings in his nose and ears, and his greasy hair tied in a ponytail. Even though it was late in the day he carried a large Styrofoam container of coffee – without a top. The steaming brown liquid sloshed back and forth with the swaying of the car. Winston tried to make himself smaller to avoid getting the hot liquid spilled on him. The blond, oblivious to Winston's discomfort, swept his arm up in a wide gesture each time he took a sip, the arc of his swing coming perilously close to Winston's chest.

"You know you really don't have to put up with this," Gran Gran said.

"What do you expect me to do?"

"Well, for starters, you could tell this ass to stop swinging that coffee so close to you, and you could remind him he's not even supposed to be drinking on the train. Hell fire, Boy, you outweigh him by at least twenty pounds. You don't have to be scared of him."

"I am not scared of him. I just don't like having public altercations. Anyway, I'm sure he knows he's not supposed to eat or drink on the train. The sign is only a few feet from his face, and it's pretty hard to miss. It's pretty obvious he doesn't care, and my telling him would only start an argument."

Gran Gran stretched herself to her full

twelve inches and snorted. *"Dammit, if you want something done, you have to do it yourself, I guess."* She squinted at the blond, wiggled her fingers and wrinkled her nose.

The blond was just taking a sip. "Ouch!" He yelled and jerked the coffee away from his lips, sloshing some on his hands. "Ouch," he said as the hot liquid burned his hand. "Damn, that's hot." His thin lips were bright red and his eyes were watery.

Gran Gran wrinkled her nose again. The blond looked startled. He looked down into the container. A look of puzzlement creased his face. He stuck his finger into the cup. Winston looked and his brown face also took on a puzzled look. Where before there'd been hot brown liquid with steam wafting up from it, there was now a dull brown chunk of . . . ice. Gran Gran chuckled.

"What the . . . ," the man said, his eyes widening. "How in the hell . . ."

"Hah! Now, let's see him drink any more of that."

Winston chuckled softly, earning him a glare from the blond. Gran Gran wiggled her fingers, and the glare turned to confusion as steam began billowing up from the brown block of ice and it puddled back into liquid form. Winston smiled. It was nice for a change to see someone else on the receiving end of trouble.

When the train pulled into Farragut North station, the blond nearly ran from the car, pitching his coffee container into the first trash can he came to. He dashed for the escalator as if he was being pursued.

Now that, Winston thought, was a neat trick. *"Thanks, Gran Gran,"* he thought at her. *"That was pretty neat."*

"Yeah, it was, wasn't it? And, it felt good too. You know, I think I know how I'm going to help you, Winston Lee."

Chapter 8

Winston wanted to ask her what she had in mind, but thought better of it. If it was shocking, his expression would show it, and he'd had enough on the morning commute. Better, he thought, to find out in the privacy of his house.

He still hesitated, and felt strange, whenever he thought about his residence as 'his' house. It *was* his home. He'd grown up there, and most of his meager fond memories were centered there. But, the deed to the place was still in his parents' names.

They hadn't lived in it for more than ten years. Around the time of Winston's thirtieth birthday, they'd simply announced that they were tired of freezing their rear ends off in winter, so they were moving to Florida. And, just like that, they up and left. Winston's father told him that he'd be getting the house when they passed away, so he wouldn't bother changing the deed. But, he warned him not to forget to pay the property taxes on time, so that there would be no problems with the state of Maryland, and to take care of the yard to keep the Homeowners' Association at bay.

They hadn't been back even once during the ten years, and he'd only visited them in Florida four or five times. They lived in a condo in Ft. Lauderdale that was close to the beach, with a great view. Winston had been thrown by the large population of elderly people in the condo and the bronzed, bikini-clad women on the beach. Both groups bothered, for much the same reason – he could never think of anything to say to either. The old people bored him, and the girls scared him to death. He ended up staying all day in his parents' condo watching cartoons and old movies on TV. His mother and father mostly just ignored him, not even inviting him to accompany them when they went out in the evenings. He also notices that after his first visit, they stopped inviting their neighbors over to introduce him.

On her way out the door, and they went out almost every evening, his mother would say, "Winston, honey, there's a TV dinner in the freezer, so just fix yourself something if you get hungry. Just leave the dirty dishes in the sink. I'll get them tomorrow. Don't wait up for us. We're likely to be late."

His father just grunted something unintelligible as he held the door, waiting for her to finish her instructions.

It had been more than five years since his

last visit. He hadn't made a conscious decision; he just hadn't made plans to go back. He didn't think his parents even noticed.

His mother wrote him once a month, always around the first of the month, and she never mentioned him visiting. She also sent him gifts at Christmas and on his birthday, always the same thing, a new shirt, which was inevitably too small for him to wear. The closet in the spare bedroom upstairs was packed with shirts he could never wear, but that he'd never taken the time to take to the store and exchange.

As he tripped over the box the FedEx delivery guy had left in front of the door, he remembered – today was his birthday.

He picked the box up, and, holding it under his left arm, took his house key out of his pocket with his right. The package and his briefcase made such a clumsy load he dropped the key in the cactus plant in the big ceramic pot just to the right of the door, and pricked his fingers retrieving it. He'd been promising himself to find a way to get rid of the darned thing, but kept putting it off, fearing that the day after he did would be the day his mother would decide to visit. The cactus, for reasons he'd never understood, was her favorite plant. If he got rid of it, she wouldn't say anything, but she'd give him one of her 'Oh dear, Winston's done it again' looks. It wouldn't do any good to replace it with a plant without spines or thorns. His mother was attached to her 'things,' and never liked getting rid of them – nor did she accept substitutes. So, the cactus stayed, and Winston was jabbed by it at least once a month.

He sucked the little bead of blood off his finger and then unlocked the door. Once inside, he bumped it shut with his buttocks and put the package on the table near the entrance along with his briefcase and the house key. There was a three-day-old pile of mail there that he'd been promising himself he'd open and read. He looked from the package to the pile. *I'll get to the mail later. No sense opening the package.* He recognized his mother's handwriting. *It'll just be a shirt or a pair of pajamas.* Next to buying him shirts, his mother loved to buy pajamas. Over the years, he'd acquired quite a collection. For some reason, she always bought the right size pajama, but insisted on patterns that were more appropriate for a ten-year-old. Winston always feared he'd be wearing a pair of Flintstone's pajamas and a burglar would break in and see him. He would never live that down. The pajamas went into the same closet as the shirts.

Winston never wore pajamas anyway. He hadn't since graduating from high school and joining the Air Force. Like his fellow recruits, he slept in his skivvies. Winston liked that. No problem with deciding what to sleep in.

White tee shirt and white undies. Just grab the top item in the drawer. At the end of the day, take off your outer clothes and hop into bed. The next morning, take them off and toss them in the hamper and grab another set. He liked the consistency.

The closet, though, was becoming a problem. It was so packed with gift boxes, the aluminum doors were beginning to bulge outward. He worried that if didn't find a new storage place, the doors were burst, and he'd have to call a repairman. He hated having to do that. Hated the way tradespeople like plumbers and electricians looked snottily at him when he had to call someone in to unplug a clogged drain. He'd tried to unclog the kitchen sink himself one time, but ended up with the little metal snake getting stuck in the pipe. The plumber he called had had to remove the snake first, and he kept chuckling to himself as he worked. All Winston could do was stand helplessly by looking on.

He shook himself like a dog coming out of a bath. He kept promising himself he'd at least change the situation about all the shirts and pajamas, give them to Goodwill or something, but like his promise to ask for a raise or to clear the weeds in the back yard, he never did anything.

The back yard was one of the unkept promises he felt bad about, but the back yard was one of his least favorite places. After his father took the fence down, the woods behind the house had begun encroaching upon the yard. One day, while playing on the deck, Winston had seen what looked like a large black snake slithering through the ankle-high grass from the direction of the forest. He'd run screaming into the house, and that was it for him as far as the back yard was concerned. It didn't help when his father explained that black snakes weren't poisonous, and were in fact good to have around because they ate rats. A snake was a snake, and as far as Winston was concerned, there was no such thing as a *good* snake. Fortunately for him, the neighbors on each side had high fences. They couldn't see into his yard to complain, and the inspectors from the Homeowners' Association would have to actually enter the premises to see the back yard. Since he'd received no complaints, he did nothing. He felt guilty about the state of the yard, but that wasn't enough to actually do anything.

In the kitchen he went straight to the refrigerator. He took out a can of Heineken, a hunk of provolone, and a plastic container of bread slices. He took out two slices of bread and popped them in the toaster on the counter near the sink. He closed the container and put it back in the fridge. He'd learned that little trick from his grandmother – keeping the bread on ice kept it longer.

From the pantry, he took out a large jar of

crunchy peanut butter, and when the toaster popped up the two slices of bread, now golden brown, he proceeded to make a peanut butter and cheese sandwich. What he'd really wanted was a fried Spam and peanut butter sandwich, but he'd forgotten to go by the Kwikee Mart for Spam. *Oh well, at least I have enough beer.*

He put the sandwich on a paper plate and put the plate and beer on a lacquer tray that his mother had brought back from a trip to Hawaii when he was thirteen. It was part of a Japanese tea ceremony set, but the teapot and cups had long since disappeared, so Winston just used it as a TV tray.

He went into the breakfast nook just off the kitchen, and sat down facing the small color TV set on the other side of the table. He reached over and switched it on, turning it to the local news channel. He then popped the tab on the Heineken and took a long swallow, letting the cold brew slide down his throat. It helped a little to wash away the accumulated frustration of the day. He took another swallow, draining the can. He got up and went back to the fridge and got another, popping the tab on the way back to the table. He put the can down and took a small bite of the sandwich, chewing slowly. *Darn, it would taste so much better with Spam.* He washed it down with more beer.

His mind drifted, as it often did when he ate. He remembered back when he'd been a relatively new employee at Advantage Consulting. Megan, who'd been hired a few months before him, stopped by his cubicle one day around lunch time to say hello. In an effort to cut back on expenses, Winston had decided to pack his lunch. That day, he had a peanut butter, grape jelly, and fried Spam sandwich, a bag of cheese curls, and a root beer. Just as she walked up, he unwrapped the sandwich. Megan took one look, made a gulping sound, and, with her hand over her mouth, fled back to her own cubicle. She never mentioned it again, but that was the last time he packed his own lunch, preferring to grab something from one of the fast food joints that were dotted around Chinatown like measles.

Winston sighed as he remembered. Megan was so darned nice. He thought how nice it would have been if he could celebrate his birthday with her. But, here he was; alone again, starring at a small color TV screen; one year older, and not a whole lot wiser.

"Happy birthday to me," he said, lifting his beer can in a toast to his tiny image on the TV screen. The image sadly toasted back.

Then, he wondered where his grandmother – or her spirit – was. He hadn't thought about her for at least an hour. Maybe she'd like to celebrate with him.

At that very moment, as if she'd read his mind again, she popped into view, hovering a few inches above the table, and blocking his view of the television.

"That's right, hon, happy birthday. I forgot to wish you that this morning," she said. "Sorry I don't have a present for you, but there's no money or shops in the spirit world. I'll have to think of something else to give you." She pointed at the small pockets in the tiny gingham dress she wore. "Besides, even if we had money or shops, I couldn't carry much in these."

"That's okay, Gran Gran. You don't need to buy me anything. I'm just glad you're here." As he said it, he realized that he meant it.

"You always were such a sweet boy. Of all my grandchildren, you're my favorite . . . were my favorite . . . oh, hell, still *are* my favorite. That's why I have to help you get your life together."

He shook his head. Fat chance of that, he thought.

"Fat chance of that," he said.

"Now, you stop that, Winston Lee," she said. "You can do whatever you set your mind to. Don't you remember me always telling you that when you were little?"

Of course he remembered. Just because he remembered it, and she'd said it, and maybe even believed it herself, didn't make it so. Those things worked for other people. Not for Winston Lee Nesbitt, born loser who had never done anything that remotely resembled success in his entire life. Losing was about the only thing he'd ever been good at. He was, in fact, just about the best loser on the planet. He could at least brag about that, if he'd been the type given to bragging, which he wasn't.

"Look, Gran Gran, I have a good job. Well, maybe it's not such a good job, but it's a steady job. The pay's not too great, but it's okay. It pays the bills, and I have a little bit left over for incidentals. My needs aren't extravagant, so that little bit is sufficient." He looked down at his half-finished beer. "I don't have a lot of technical skills. I'm just good at numbers and patterns. I never went back to college to finish my degree after I got out of the service, and I'm not too comfortable with people, so I wouldn't even be good working in a fast food joint. My life is what it is, and I think I just have to accept it. By the way . . . could you please stand on the table, or sit on something? Watching you floating in the air like that is kinda freaking me out."

She drifted down until it looked like her tiny feet were in contact with the table cloth. She made no sound, didn't ruffle the cloth, and since she cast no shadow, it was hard to tell.

"There," she said. "Is that better? Now, Winston Lee, you have got to quit being so negative. You can do better. You *will* do better if I have anything to say about it, and I do believe I have something to say about it."

Winston's eyebrows shot up. "Like-"

"Like, I'm a spirit now," she interrupted him with a wave of her tiny hand and a severe frown. His lips snapped shut. "I'm new at this, but I've learned that we spirits have abilities you ordinary mortals lack – you've seen some of them." Winston's head bobbed up and down. "Of course, it's not all fun and games. Did you know, for instance, we can't dream? We don't need sleep, so there's no need for dreaming. Fact is, I miss both. I like taking a little nap now and then." Her face had a wistful look. "Another thing, Boy; I'm your grandmother, and you're supposed to do what I say. Got it?"

"And, what do you think a 12-inch gho-, er, spirit can do to make *my* life better?"

She frowned at him again. "I thought you'd never ask, Boy." Her frown changed to a wicked looking smile, and she rubbed her hands together. "Sit back and enjoy your sandwich and beer, and I'll tell you what I'm gonna do."

Charles Ray

"Sic semper tyrannis!" - **John Wilkes Booth**

Chapter 9
■■■

Winston slept well that night.

Considering what his grandmother had told him just before he went to bed, he should, by rights, have tossed and turned all night.

After he'd finished his supper, they moved to the living room. He sat on the sofa, and she sat, or sort of hovered, in the big chair across the coffee table from him. They talked until well after midnight – actually, she did most of the talking, while he sat there with his eyes wide and his mouth agape. He wasn't sure he believed she could do everything she said she could, but after watching her demonstration with the obnoxious guy with the coffee on the subway, he thought it might *just* be possible. Even if it didn't work it might be fun to watch.

It was with that thought in mind that he

drifted off to sleep.

Most people who live in the suburbs prefer having wooded lots, or living near the woods. They like the sounds of nature. Winston tolerated it.

The chirping and clacking of birds and other creatures late at night and first thing in the morning did not make him feel any waves of pleasure. They scared him. Often at night he'd lie awake wondering what kind of creature was making those sounds, and whether or not they might be dangerous. In the morning, the chorus started with the first annoying buzz of his alarm clock, as if the alarm woke the denizens of the forest as well.

It began at 5:30 am. First came the insistent buzzing of the alarm. Then, immediately afterwards, the clacking, chattering and croaking from the dense stand of trees behind his house. For once, though, it didn't bother him.

He came awake slowly, reluctant to leave the pleasant dream he'd been having. A failure with the opposite sex in daylight, in his dreams he was a completely different person.

The first sight to greet him when his vision finally cleared was his grandmother, floating a few inches from his face.

"Grack, guh, eek!" He quickly pulled the sheets over his face. At the same time, he realized that the after effect of his dream was still glaringly pleasant. He quickly rolled onto his side, hoping she hadn't noticed. Then, he had a shocking thought. *What if she can see my dreams!*

When his heart stopped pounding, and he could breathe evenly again, he slowly eased the sheet down from his eyes, peering at her over the hem.

"I wish you wouldn't do that, Gran Gran," he said. "You almost caused me to have a heart attack. Can't you wait outside my bedroom until I wake up . . . like a normal person? I mean . . . I know you're not a *normal,* or anything, just a, well . . . oh, never mind. Could you just not be hovering over me when I wake up?"

She drifted lazily to his left and settled on the rumpled bed cover.

"Sorry, hon," she said. "But, you looked so peaceful sleeping. I just wanted to look at you. You remember I told you I don't sleep or dream. Well, it's sort of nice watching you do it. And, from the look of that sheet before you turned over, you were having a really pleasant dream." She giggled and rolled her eyes. Winston's cheeks felt hot.

Winston held the sheet against his chest as he levered himself into a sitting position, his back against the headboard and his legs crossed in an effort to conceal the fact that he hadn't yet 'recovered' from his dream.

"Uh, Gran Gran, I'm still getting used to you being here. I've about come to terms with it, but, having you pop up floating around like this all over the place, and at the oddest times, is a bit hard to deal with. You're going to have to take it slow with me, okay? Especially first thing in the morning."

"Okay, I'll keep that in mind. Now, you hurry up and get yourself dressed. We've got a long and interesting day ahead of us." Then, with a 'poof' she was gone.

After waiting a few seconds, Winston reached under the sheets and scratched his crotch, which became dry and itchy when he slept. He then pulled the covers aside and eased out of bed. He padded to the bathroom where he brushed his teeth, shaved, and showered, looking over his shoulder constantly to see if his grandmother had decided to come back unannounced.

Notwithstanding the fact that she'd changed his diapers and dressed him when he was a kid, having her witness his morning tumescence was a bit unsettling. It didn't matter that she was not a real living being – she was *there*, and the thought made him cringe.

After he finished showering, he found a clean set of underwear in his drawer and got dressed. Just before pulling on his trousers, though, he smeared a generous amount of calamine lotion on his inner thighs to soothe the itch, a legacy of the one time he'd gone camping.

During his basic training after joining the

Air Force, Winston's training sergeants decided it would be a good idea if the young airmen understood what life was like for the other services, like the Army and Marine Corps, so they took them on a three-day bivouac in the hills near Lackland Air Force Base in San Antonio, Texas. They hadn't taken into account that even in central Texas, the summer heat is oppressive, and the mosquitos are the size of humming birds. What Winston got from the three-day nightmare was a severe case of crotch fungus that recurred from time to time, infected mosquito bites on his arms and legs, and an intense aversion to anything having to do with the outdoors. The crotch rash was so severe, he had to walk bow legged for a month.

His dislike of the outdoors wasn't confined to camping. He also hated picnics. Shortly after starting work at Advantage, one of his co-workers suggested that everyone get together one day for lunch and have a picnic in a park a few blocks from the office. Winston had joined them for the first twenty minutes or so, but the sight of used condoms in the short grass at the park entrance, and the two winos sleeping a few feet from where they were planning to eat were more than he could stomach. When no one was paying attention, he sneaked off, and then went and had the 5-piece fried chicken special at a Popeye's not far away. There'd been office picnics a few times since, but thankfully, the organizers always neglected to invite him.

As he exited the bathroom, he thought about the conversation he'd had with his grandmother.

Her plan was simple, or so it had seemed when she presented it to him. All he had to do was to confront anyone who gave him a problem, to stand up for himself. If he couldn't handle it himself, Gran Gran would do her little finger waving, nose crinkling thing, and give the malefactor what for. After seeing what she'd done to the guy with the coffee, Winston had no doubt she could wreak havoc, but she'd also confessed that this whole spirit with magic powers thing was new to her, and she was still working some kinks out of it. When he pressed her for details, she just shrugged and told him not to worry. Ordinarily, he would have worried. He would have lain awake all night worrying. For some reason, he hadn't. Sure, things could go wrong. In Winston's life something was always going wrong. But, for a change, he didn't worry about it.

For the first time in a long time, he was looking forward to the morning commute, looking forward to finding out what his grandmother could do. He knew, for instance, that Leland Carter would find some reason to give him grief. He was, in fact, almost looking forward to it. *Gran Gran will show him what's what.* He hoped.

After finishing his morning toilet, Winston dressed in a dark blue suit, a pastel blue shirt and a red 'power' tie with thin white stripes. He spent extra time buffing his shoes to a high gloss, smiling at his reflection in the toes. That's how great he felt. It was as if he was someone else.

It was nearly 7:00 when he finally went downstairs to the kitchen. Ordinarily he would be rushing out of the house at that time to catch the bus. He decided that this morning he'd take the time to have a decent breakfast for a change. He had toast with blueberry jam, a piece of Swiss cheese, and a cup of instant coffee, which was better than the bagel and deli coffee he usually wolfed down as he dashed down the street toward his building. He sat at the table, taking his time, and enjoying it more than any breakfast he could remember.

As he was rinsing his coffee cup in the sink, Gran Gran popped into view front of him, just above the window sill behind the sink. She had a wicked smile on her elfin face.

"Ready to go?" she asked.

"As ready as I'll ever be," he responded, and with an uncharacteristic swing in his step, he headed for the bus stop.

Luckily, when the 7:49 bus arrived, it wasn't crowded, so Winston was able to get a seat in front just behind the driver. Gran Gran perched quietly on his shoulder for the entire ride.

The Shady Grove Metro Station, on the other hand, was crowded. The late morning commuter rush was just starting. Winston knew he would have to scramble for a seat despite this being the first station on the Shady Grove-Glenmont line.

He wasn't sure what his grandmother was doing, but as he moved from the bus stop to and through the station, she was continually waving her fingers, wrinkling her nose, and squinting her eyes. The only result of this he could see was, like Moses parting the Red Sea, the crowd parted as he approached. Many people, in fact, seemed to be moving with alacrity to get out of his way.

For a change he had no problems getting his ticket from the dispenser. He remembered to insert it correctly at the turnstile, earning a smile and a thumb up from the station manager.

No one tried pushing past him at the turnstile or on the escalator, and he wasn't jostled on the platform. When the train arrived and the doors *whooshed* open, and he waited patiently while the few passengers exited the car, no one tried to shove him out of the way to get on, meaning that he was the first to board the now empty car. He got one of the inward facing seats near the center, and until the Twinbrook Station, two stops down the line, had the seat all to himself.

When the train pulled jerkily into

Twinbrook, and the doors slid open, about a third of the passengers in Winston's car got off. Among the boarding passengers was a middle aged, obese man wearing an overcoat despite the warm weather. There were several empty seats in the car, but the man decided that he wanted to sit next to Winston.

One couldn't call Winston fat – he was more on the stocky side, and a bit broad in the hips, so he fully occupied his half of the seat. The man in the overcoat was considerably broader in the hips than Winston. He had to wiggle his huge buttocks to squeeze in to the space next to Winston. His actions were acccmpanied by a bit of grunting, and resulted in Winston being jammed tightly against the Plexiglass barrier. The man glared sideways at Winston as he squeezed him against the immovable barrier, a look that seemed to say, "There's not enough room here for both of us, why don't you move?"

Up till now, Winston hadn't really felt any weight from his grandmother's incorporeal form. But, now, he could feel her vibrating. A quick glance showed him that her caramel colored cheeks had two bright red spots, and her brows were knitted with anger.

On any other day, Winston would have quietly ignored the man. Not, however, on this day. Now was the time to put his grandmother's plan to the test.

"You know, Sir," he said quietly. "I really

don't think this seat is adequate for two gentlemen of our size."

The man turned his head and glared directly at Winston. The glare was accompanied by a dank odor like onions and dirty sweat socks. He wiggled his buttocks again, squeezing his left thigh against Winston. He raised his buttocks slightly, and there was a sound like paper tearing, followed almost immediately by a strong, biting odor that brought tears to Winston's eyes.

"Sir," Winston said again, in a firmer voice this time. "I said, there's not enough room on this seat for the two of us."

"If it's too uncomfortable," the man said. "Why don't you move?"

There was another paper-ripping sound, and another vicious assault upon Winston's olfactory senses. He pinches his nostrils shut, but it didn't help.

"Don't you worry, Winston Lee. I'll take care of this one."

She clenched her eyes shut and wiggled her nose. Next to him, Winston heard the fat man mutter, "Urp." Then he placed his pudgy hands over his bulging belly and leaned forward. Winston could feel his body quivering.

"Oooh, urp, Jesus Christ," the man muttered. "What the hell! Oooh!"

There were more sounds of paper tearing, accompanied by little bubbling noises.

Passengers in nearby seats were looking at the fat man with expressions of distaste, that is, those who hadn't clamped their hands over their noses to try and shut out the fetid odor coming from beneath him.

The man clamped his beefy legs together and rocked back and forth. His face contorted in pain, and his nose wrinkled as the gassy odor he was emitting began to get to even him. His fleshy lips quivered and he put his hand over his nose.

"Oh, God," he whispered in a raspy, pleading voice. "What's happening to me?" God didn't answer him. It was Gran Gran at the helm for this ride, and she was clearly having too much fun to stop and answer the poor guy.

The smell was now so strong, that Winston was reluctant to open his mouth. *Goodness gracious, that's disgusting! How do proctologists deal with having to peer into orifices that emit that kind of smell?*

Despite the discomfort, though, Winston found himself perversely enjoying the man's situation. He was careful not to let it show on his face. He sat quietly, with a blank look on his face, still pinching his nostrils shut, trying to look as if nothing out of the ordinary was happening. For once, people were giving him sympathetic looks.

When the train pulled into White Flint Station, the man heaved up from the seat and bolted toward the door, not even waiting for them to open completely before squeezing through. Everyone watched with relieved smiles on their faces as he waddled quickly across the platform toward the escalator, one hand over his stomach, the other over the seat of his pants, which showed a large, dark, oval stain.

One part of Winston felt sorry for the man. Another part exulted in seeing him get his comeuppance. For once, it wasn't Winston on the receiving end of public humiliation, and it felt good. The other passengers smiled and nodded at him, happy to see the obnoxious man get what he deserved. Winston smiled back, but tried to look sympathetic. No sense in publicly gloating – at least not outwardly.

"That was fantastic, Gran Gran. What did you do to him?"

"Let's just say he's gonna need to change his pants and underwear before he gets back on the train. I feel sorry for the taxi driver that takes him back home to change, but I bet he thinks twice about trying to push anybody around on the subway. Her lopsided grin told Winston that she'd enjoyed what she'd done as much as he'd enjoyed witnessing it.

He clapped a hand over his mouth and coughed to mask a laugh. *This is pretty neat. Maybe having a little spirit of a grandmother around won't be so bad after all.*

The opening and closing of the train doors, helped by the ventilation system, soon cleared most of the foul odor from the car. The few passengers that boarded looked around and made faces at the little that lingered. Winston smiled, and sat back to enjoy the rest of his commute.

Chapter 10

The rest of the commute was uneventful. Winston surprised himself when he realized that he found it boring and disappointing. He'd enjoyed seeing his grandmother inflict pain upon an ass that richly deserved it – and then felt shocked that he'd even thought of the man as an 'ass.' He was looking forward to the next confrontation.

As a child Winston had never indulged in the cruel things other children did. He'd never pulled the wings from flies – he'd never touched a fly. The small animals that roamed his neighborhood were safe from him. He didn't tie cans to the tails of cats, or give dogs pepper-laced meat. The truth was, he was afraid of them, so he avoided them. Whenever he saw other kids tormenting a cat or squirrel, he'd run home crying. In high school, he'd gotten a D in biology because he refused to dissect the frog that had placed before him in lab class. In fact, he'd thrown up all over the lab bench and the kids to either side of him.

He hadn't owned a pet hamster. He did keep a gold fish for a few months, but when he found it floating on top of the water one day, he'd soured on pets from that point on. He never collected insects. The thought of pushing a pin through something, even bugs that were already dead, was more than he could handle.

The fact that he could actually have enjoyed seeing another person suffer, even one who deserved it, gave him a twinge of guilt, albeit only a momentary one. He felt powerful for the first time in his life.

It was almost 9:00 when he got off the elevator on his floor. Leland Carter, his foot tapping on the floor, was waiting at Winston's cubicle. He had his chest out and his shoulders back in an effort to look tall, but still had to look up at Winston. He had his arm draped over the cubicle wall, and had a vulpine smile on his face.

Winston was briefly taken aback. His nerves almost broke, but he shook himself and continued to advance toward his boss.

"I hope you have a good reason for

being so late," Carter said. His tone said he actually hoped that Winston didn't have a good reason.

"Well," Winston said. "I guess that depends. I decided to have breakfast at home this morning, so that made me miss my usual buss, and once you get on the Metro, you're pretty stuck. You can only go as fast as the trains run."

If Winston had kicked Carter in the crotch he wouldn't have gotten a better reaction. The man recoiled as if he'd been struck, and glared up at Winston with a degree of malevolence that on any other day would have sent Winston fleeing for the men's room.

"You did what?" Carter asked. His eyes were wide.

"I think I spoke quite clearly," Winston said. "I decided to have breakfast at home this morning, so I'm running a bit late. Was that clear enough? Or, would you like for me to repeat it?"

Carter's face turned as red as Winston's tie. His eyes got buggy and looked as if they'd pop out of the sockets. His lips moved, but no words came out of his mouth, just a little dribble of spit. Ordinarily a sight like this would have caused Winston, a rather fastidious person at times, to feel a bit queasy. Instead, he found himself enjoying it. It was the first time he'd ever bested Carter in a verbal battle, and it felt good. It felt *damned* good.

Finally, Carter recovered a bit. He took a deep breath. "Nesbitt, we need to talk in my office." He then brushed past Winston and marched toward his office.

Winston waited a few moments, long enough to make sure Carter knew he wasn't hot on his heels like an obedient dog, and then he followed. He knew this would further infuriate the little man.

Once they were inside the office, Carter closed the door, and walked slowly around his desk. He took his time sitting in the big leather chair, leaning back and playing with the gold Cross pen he kept near his inbox, all the while looking up at Winston. He hadn't invited Winston to sit, and one of his rules was that no one sat in his office unless invited to do so. Winston walked to the visitor chair that was placed squarely in front of the desk across from Carter. He moved it slightly to the side and sat. Carter's eyebrows lifted half an inch. He opened his mouth, then snapped it shut.

"Go ahead and tell the pompous little jackass what you think of him," Gran Gran said.

Before Winston could speak, Carter shook his head and leaned forward. "What's gotten into you Nesbitt?" he asked. "Don't you like this job?"

"Is that a trick question? Actually, I like the job fine. No, actually, I guess I don't like it very much at all, but what I really don't like is the way I'm treated around here."

"That's telling him," his grandmother said. *"Stand up for your rights like a man."*

Carter's face had a surprised look. "Just what exactly is wrong with the way you're treated?"

"Oh, come on, Leland." Winston said. Carter's shocked look pleased him. "You're always on my back, making me change reports again and again. Insulting me every chance you get. Hell, *everything* is wrong with the way I'm treated here. You, for instance, are very disrespectful, and it has to stop. It has to stop right *now.*"

"Oh really, and what if it doesn't stop? Just how do you propose to make it stop? I am, after all, your boss, or have you forgotten? The way it works is, I give the orders and you obey, not the other way around."

"What a ninny," Gran Gran said. *"I'll bet even his mother dislikes him. Okay, Winston Lee, since he doesn't seem to want to be reasonable, it's time for me to take over. You remember what I told you to say?"*

Winston nodded. He smiled. "No, Leland, I haven't forgotten that you're the boss," he said. "But, if you don't apologize to me for the crappy way you treat me, and promise to stop it right now and never do it again, something bad, and I mean really bad, is going to happen to you. Refuse to apologize and I want be responsible for the consequences."

Carter laughed. "Oh, really now? And just what bad thing is going to happen? You wouldn't be threatening me by any chance, would you, Nesbitt?"

Winston wanted very much to wipe the smug look off his face. "Threatening? No, I wouldn't exactly call it threatening. Actually, I'm just stating simple facts. Actions have consequences, and when we do bad things, bad things come back to us. You have been very bad, and if you don't immediately make amends, you will have to pay. And, I can promise you, the payment won't be pleasant."

"That's telling him, Winston Lee."

"Okay, Gran Gran, give it to him." Winston smiled at Carter. "Don't say I didn't warn you. You had your chance and you blew it, so now you have to see what happens to bullies who refuse to reform."

His grandmother wiggled her nose, waggled her fingers, and scrunched up her eyes. There were no sounds, but Carter's reaction was instantaneous, and amazing to watch.

First, he bent at the waist and grabbed at his stomach. His face screwed up in a painful expression, with his eyes round and looking like they wanted to pop out of the sockets. He made little gurgling sounds in his throat, and Winston could hear bubbling sounds coming from his stomach.

"Ooh, ooh," he said, whimpering like a

puppy in pain. "I don't feel so good. What's happening?"

"I told you, if you don't apologize and promise never to pick on me again, you'll just keep feeling bad. In fact, you might even feel worse." *Frankly, I hope you refuse to apologize. I'm enjoying this.*

"Now, now, Winston Lee, that's not very Christian of you."

"Sorry, Gran Gran, but he has been such a mean person, I can't help it."

"Just kidding, Hon, this ass doesn't deserve Christian charity."

Carter looked at him, disbelief warring with discomfort for a facial expression. Had it been anyone else, Winston might have been moved by his suffering. For all the years that Winston had worked at Advantage Consulting, though, Carter had tormented and insulted him on a daily basis. He deserved to suffer a bit. Winston just sat there, his arms folded across his chest, a placid expression on his face.

"Wha . . ., I don't, uh, oh." Carter's face was beginning to turn blue.

"It's just going to get worse unless you apologize," Winston said. "Trust me. Just apologize and promise to change your behavior, and the pain will stop."

"H-how . . . how do you know this?"

"I just know."

Carter looked like he was in agony. He clutched at his stomach, and groaned and whimpered. Winston could hear a rumbling sound from his midsection.

"It must be something I had for breakfast this morning," he said. "Maybe the orange juice was a little off, or the bacon was rancid, and I didn't notice it. You wait right here, Nesbitt, until I get back. I'm not finished with you."

There was no real conviction in his voice, and he avoided touching Winston as he came from behind his desk and headed for the door. Once outside, he didn't even bother closing the door before making a dash in the direction of the executive bathroom as fast as his wobbly legs could carry him.

"Wait right here, Winston Lee," Gran Gran said. *"I'm gonna go make sure he gets the point."*

"You're not going to do anything dangerous or really harmful, are you?"

"Of course not . . . well, at least I don't think so. Stop worrying, a little case of the trots never killed anyone."

Winston waited patiently as instructed and about ten minutes later Carter returned. He looked pale, and beads of sweat dotted his forehead. His comb over had gone askew, and the limp strands were plastered to his brow. His partially bald pate glistened with sweat, and was streaked darker pink where the comb over hadn't kept the sun from tanning it. For once, he didn't bother to brush the stray hair back into place. He no longer looked as pained as he had when he rushed out.

"Like I said, must have been something I ate," he said, but his voice lacked conviction. He eyed Winston warily as he circled around him to make his way behind the protective barrier of his desk.

"Or," Winston said. "It could be that you didn't apologize to me for the nasty way you've been treating me since I came to work here, and you suffered just like I said you would."

"Are you trying to tell me that if I don't apologize, I'll get sick again? Do you seriously expect me to believe that you can control the way I feel?"

"Yes, as a matter of fact, that's precisely what I'm saying." Winston crossed his fingers behind his back. He'd expected his grandmother would have convinced Carter to do the right thing while he was in the toilet, but apparently she hadn't. "Actually, it's not me controlling how you feel," he said. "You might say it's your guilty conscience that's doing it. You could call it any number of things, but the thing is, if you don't a0pologize for the lousy way you've treated me, and promise never to do it again, you're going to get sick again, and this time it'll be a whole lot worse."

Gran Gran popped into view. She had a big smile on her face and her head was bobbing up and down in the affirmative.

"That's a load of hooey," Carter said. He puffed his chest out and put his hands on his hips, staring up at Winston. "Bring it on. Nesbitt, you've done and said a lot of crazy things since you started working here, but this takes the cake." He laughed, but weakly.

"Well, I tried to warn you," Winston said. *"I think he needs another demonstration, Gran Gran."*

"Thought you'd never ask. I was gonna zap him in the john, but I didn't have any way to talk to him, so it wouldn't have worked." She laughed, and then scrunched up her eyes and wiggled her fingers.

Carter doubled over as if he'd been kicked in the stomach. His face turned red, and his eyes got all wide and watery. A loud sound like paper tearing came from behind him, and a noxious odor filled the office. He groaned and squealed. Winston pinched his nostrils shut to block out the odor.

"Oh, my goodness, Gran Gran, you're not making him do what that man on the subway did, are you?"

"No, I'm must making him feel like that's what's happening. You can bet he'll make a quick trip to the toilet to check his undies. He'll be a bit surprised to find nothing . . . well, he might find a little something. Can't be completely sure. I'm still working the bugs out of this one."

Carter held his hands up in supplication. "Okay, okay," he said. "I'm sorry for the way I treated you."

"And, you promise never to be mean to me again?"

"Yeah, yeah," Carter said. "I promise to treat you nice from here on out. Now, make it stop! Please! Make it stop!"

Winston looked at his grandmother, who smiled, winked and waved her hand. Carter got a funny look on his face. He straightened up, letting his hands fall to his sides. He took a deep breath and rubbed his stomach. He refused to look Winston in the eye. Instead, he looked around the office as if he expected someone or something to jump out of a corner at him. Then, he remembered to push his comb over back into place. He kept looking behind, and feeling tentatively at the back of his trousers.

"Is there anything else you need from me?" Winston asked. "I have a couple of reports I need to get done today."

Carter waved his hands without looking at Winston. "No, I don't need anything else. Go ahead." He looked relieved as Winston left his office, and continued to peer around.

Two things happened as Winston walked back toward his cubicle. Carter pushed past him, walking stiffly, heading in the direction of the executive washroom, and he bumped into Megan who was just turning away from the copy machine.

"Oh, sorry, Winston," she said. "I was making some copies, and I guess I wasn't paying attention."

Winston noticed that her hands were empty, and that the copy machine was located close enough to Carter's office that someone with sharp hearing could hear what was going on inside. He also noticed that Megan was beaming at him.

"Sure," he said. "No problem."

"Is everything okay?" She looked from him to Carter who was just disappearing through the washroom door. The look of concern that was on her face when she looked at Winston changed to a half smile when she looked at Carter.

"Everything's fine," he said. "Say, would you like to have lunch with me today?"

She looked at him with wide-eyed surprise. It was the first time he'd ever initiated an invitation. His temerity even surprised him.

"Of course, Winston," she said. "Where would you like to go?"

"You pick the place. We can leave around noon, okay?" And, without waiting for her to answer, he strode confidently into his cubicle.

If you have to ask how much it costs, you can't afford it. –
Anonymous

Chapter 11
■■■

Back in his cubicle, Winston began sorting
the papers on his desk. Gran Gran hovered
in the center of his desk over a pile of folders
with her hands on her hips. She scowled at
Winston.

"And, just what was that all about?" Her
voice had a demanding tone.

"What was what all about?" Winston
affected an innocent look. He then put his
finger to his lips. "Oh, and keep your voice
down. Somebody might hear you."

"Don't you be playing with me, Boy. I saw
the goo goo eyes you were making at that
hussy."

"Gran Gran, Megan is *not* a hussy. She's a nice girl, the nicest girl I've ever known in fact, and I happen to like her." He didn't bother adding that she was the first girl he'd ever asked out. He still couldn't believe he'd done that.

"I told you that she is not the right girl for you," she said, stamping her tiny feet and making no sound. "I'm working on that. Why can't you just be patient and wait for me to help you?"

"I don't need your help for that, Gran Gran. There are some things I should do for myself."

She shook her head. Her nostrils flared. "Boy, you need my help for everything, especially *that*. You don't know the first thing about women. The only thing you've ever been able to do for yourself, other than feeding yourself and getting into trouble, was go to the toilet, and you were five before you could do that right."

"But, I-"

She waved her hands at him in a chopping motion. "No more arguing, Boy. Just hush up and listen to what I tell you. When I find the right woman for you, I'll let you know." Then, she disappeared again.

Winston was becoming accustomed to her presence, but her constant appearing and disappearing was unnerving, especially her habit of blinking out of sight whenever he had something important to say. While people had ignored him for most of his life, it was now starting to annoy him. And, that his grandmother of all people should do it *really* rankled.

Well, I guess I'll just have to show her that there are some things I can do for myself. I'm not about to let her chose a woman for me.

He'd had one experience with well-meaning friends trying to 'fix him up' with the opposite sex when he was in the Air Force, and it had soured him forever.

Winston's barracks mates, feeling sorry for him for hanging out at the library or in the barracks while they were out having fun, arranged a date for him with a girl in Floresville, a little town southeast of San Antonio. It had taken them two hours of intense argument to get him to agree to go along with them, and in the end, they just grabbed him by the arms and pulled him along, jamming him into Carl Levine's white Mustang, with two of them in front and two in the backseat of him on either side to keep him from getting out.

They drove for over an hour until they came to the little road house on one of the farm to market roads that crisscross Texas. With Winston still held firmly between two of them, they entered the place. Five girls sat at two tables that had been pushed together in the back corner; a white girl with blue-streaked blonde hair, two Mexican girls, and two chocolate colored black girls. They were all dressed in provocative, cleavage-displaying blouses, and mini-skirts that barely covered the essentials.

The girls smiled and waved when Winston and his four escorts approached the tables. After seating Winston between one of the black girls, Melanie something or other, and a Mexican girl named Consuela, they did boy-girl-boy-girl to seat everyone else, with Winston's two jailers seated near enough to grab him should he decide to make a run for it.

Joe Larson, one of his jailers, and the only other black guy in the group, seated himself with Melanie and the other Mexican girl flanking him. He ordered drinks, tequila with a slice of lime and *dos equis* beer chasers for everyone except Winston. For him, he ordered a large glass of lemonade. When the drinks came, everyone immediately began knocking them back, while Winston sipped gingerly at his lemonade.

After immediate thirsts were quenched, the small talk began.

"What's your name again, big fellow," Melanie asked Winston.

"Winston, Winston Nesbitt," he replied.

"Well, Winston Winston Nesbitt, what do you think of the Chuck Wagon?" She leaned forward, brushing her large breast against his shoulder and letting her hand fall lazily against his upper thigh.

"T-the w-what?" Winston asked.

"The Chuck Wagon. This place here. It's where we hang out and hook up."

Her fingers began to trace lazy circles on his thigh, causing a tingling sensation in his groin.

"Uh, uh . . . it's okay, I g-guess."

She leaned harder against him, causing him to pull back, spilling some of his lemonade on Consuela who, in turn, jerked back and spilled beer in Artie Miller's lap.

"Hey, watch it, Nesbitt," the redheaded Miller said. "You're making her spill beer on my new chinos. These things cost me a week's pay. And look at what you did to her blouse."

Consuela's blouse had a large, dark, oval spot just over her left breast. His lemonade had soaked through the white fabric, turning it transparent, and making it all too apparent that she wasn't wearing a bra. Winston grabbed a napkin and began rubbing at the spot, causing Consuela to close her eyes and make moaning noises. He didn't really notice until he felt her nipple growing larger under his hand. He jerked his hand away as if he'd been burned.

"Ooh, don't stop," Consuela said. "That felt good."

"I'm s-sorry," Winston mumbled. "I didn't mean to do that."

Melanie leaned in close, her lips almost touching Winston's ear. "I wish you'd do that to me," she whispered. He jerked his head away.

"My, my, you are the shy one," she said aloud. "Don't worry, I don't bite . . . at least, not in public." She accompanied this with a gentle squeeze of his thigh, and then moved her hand further up his leg. Despite the air conditioning being on full blast, Winston began to feel warm.

"Hey, Winston Winston, wouldn't you like to blow this joint and find some place more private?" she whispered into his ear.

"Uh, it's just one Winston," he said. "And, why would we want to leave? We just got here, and you haven't even finished your drink."

She downed the rest of the tequila in one gulp, and shoved the beer aside. "To hell with the drink," she said. "I got something else I'd rather put in my mouth." Her hand was resting on his crotch. "My, my, you *are* a big boy. Wonder what that would taste like."

The other conversations at the table had stopped. All eyes were on Winston. His face was burning. He wanted to reach down and move her hand, but everyone was watching, and he was afraid to cause a scene. He was reacting to her hand in the same way he reacted in some of his dreams. It was pleasant and unsettling at the same time, and his heart started pounding. His mouth felt dry and his tongue swollen.

"You don't talk a lot, do you, Winston?"

she said. "That's good, because I can think of a much better use for those lips of yours."

Things, Winston thought, were getting out of hand. Actually, Melanie was getting a lot into her hand, and he was scared to death that if he didn't get her hand away from his body, she'd get even more into it.

"I . . . oh . . . ooh," was all he could manage to say.

"Ooh is right, big boy," she said, and then leaned in again to whisper in his ear. "You *sure* you don't want to go somewhere and do it?"

"D-do what?" Winston asked quietly.

Her mouth dropped open. "It," she said. "The beast with two backs. Getting it on. Making out." Then, louder, she said, "Screwing. Don't you know anything? Hey, have you ever made out with a girl before?"

"No, uh, I mean, yes . . . well, uh . . . what I mean is . . ."

She clapped her hands to her face, and in a voice that could be heard all over the room, said, "Oh, my goodness, you've never done it before. You're a cherry boy!" She laughed and gave his crotch a squeeze. "What a waste of good meat."

By now, everyone at the table was laughing so hard, tears were flowing from their eyes. Those at nearby tables were staring and tittering. Tears were also flowing from Winston's eyes, but not from laughing.

Melanie seemed to be enjoying herself. "I

never had me a cherry boy before. That might be fun. Hey, one of you girls want to help me bust a cherry?" All the while she kept massaging his crotch, rubbing her breasts against his arm, and when she wasn't talking, she was sticking her tongue in his ear or licking his ear lobe. When she stuck her tongue in his ear, he jerked and knocked his lemonade over, sending the liquid splashing over the table.

That caused everyone to laugh harder. "Way to go, Nesbitt," Miller said.

"Wow," Consuela said. "The cherry boy is crying."

The laughter got louder.

It was all too much for Winston. He stood abruptly, flinging Melanie's hand from his crotch. This sent her backwards, her legs in the air and her skirt up around her waist. He stumbled toward the door without looking back, bumping into a waitress in the process and sending tankards of beer crashing to the sawdust covered floor, and splashing it over the shiny boots of a man in a large cowboy hat who'd been trying to impress a woman half his age. Winston didn't even stop to say 'excuse me.' He continued to stumble and bump his way to the door, and then outside into the dimly-lit, gravel covered parking lot. He walked until he found the car they'd come in. He looked around. No one was near. He leaned over, pressing his head against the roof of the car and let the tears flow.

Every time he remembered the incident, Winston felt heaviness in his chest and his eyes burned. He never again went out with the guys from his barracks, and they never brought the incident up – in his presence. In fact, the four of them seemed to go out of their way to avoid Winston except when it was unavoidable..

No, there's no way I'm going to let Gran Gran make decisions about my love life. His one experience with blind dating was enough. In Winston's dictionary, blind date and disaster were synonyms. He could mess up his love life without any help from anyone else.

He knew his grandmother would be disappointed, perhaps even angry, and she might give him a hard time about it, but he would just have to deal with it. He also didn't like the way she got all catty and insulting about Megan, and was determined to say something to her the next time she did it.

Charles Ray

Chapter 12

Megan picked the most expensive restaurant on F Street. He knew the moment they walked in that it was expensive, because the gilt engraved menus in the glass covered frames at the door didn't have prices for any of the items. He'd been half afraid she'd do that. The lighting was dim, and the place had a snooty air about it. It was one of those places his father always avoided. He used to say, "When I'm paying good money, I want to be treated like I'm paying good money. I do not pay to get insulted." He would never eat at a French restaurant for that reason.

"I won't even visit the country," he once said. "If the rest of the French are like the little snobs who work in restaurants here, I don't want to have anything to do with them." Winston's father was like that. Once he made his mind up about something, he never wavered. Winston had inherited that trait when it came to restaurants.

Even though the restaurant Megan had chosen wasn't French, the waiters were as snotty as those in the French restaurants Winston had seen on TV.

"Do you have a reservation, sir?" the waiter asked as soon as Winston and Megan entered.

Winston looked around. More than half the tables he could see were vacant. "No," he said. "We don't have reservations."

"I'm afraid, then, there will be at least a thirty minute wait. You may wait in the bar if you wish."

Winston opened his mouth to point out the number of empty tables, but before he could speak, the waiter turned on his heel, and, with his nose in the air, walked away.

The bar was a corner of the front of the room with a scuffed counter behind which stood a bored looking young man wearing a white jacket. Behind the scuffed counter was a tall shelf containing a wide variety of liquors and liqueurs. On the shelf that jutted out from the counter were cans and bottles of beer and soft drinks.

"Something I can get you folks?" the bored looking young man asked as Winston and Megan walked up.

Winston turned to Megan. "I'll just have a Diet Coke," she said.

"Two Cokes," Winston said. "One Diet, one Regular."

The young man dropped several tiny ice

cubes in two murky looking glasses and then filled them with a hose and spigot contraption that was in a forked holder beneath the counter. He then set them on the counter on paper coasters.

"Which one is the Diet Coke?" Megan asked.

He looked at them for a few seconds, and then grabbed one and pushed it in front of her. She picked the glass up and took a tentative sip. Satisfied that it was in fact what she'd ordered, she smiled and took another drink. The bartender, with a look of complete indifference, turned to the register and began punching buttons. The machine made whirring and clinking sounds and then spit a strip of paper from a slot on the front, which he ripped off and placed in front of Winston.

"That'll be twelve dollars," he said. "You want to pay now, or would you like to run a tab?"

Winston was just taking a sip of his drink. He sputtered when some made its way down the wrong pipe, spewing droplets of Coke over the counter. He put the glass down and wiped his lips with the back of his hand. The register receipt had drink stains on it, but the amount was clear. *My goodness, I hate to think what the food will cost.* He cleared his throat, and took his wallet out. He extracted his Visa card and handed it to the bartender. "Uh, no, that won't be necessary," he said. "I'll pay now, thanks."

The man took the card, holding it with two fingers as if it was somehow infected with some communicable disease. He turned it over and looked at the back, then held it up before his eyes as if trying to see through it. He then swiped it through the machine at the side of the register, and waited until a green light started blinking before finishing the transaction. A slip of paper oozed from the top of the machine. The bartender took it and passed it, along with a pen, to Winston, and turned his attention to wiping at the countertop with a grimy looking rag. Winston noted that in addition to the twelve dollar drink charge, amounts had been added for DC taxes and a ten percent service fee. At the bottom of the slip was a blank labeled 'Gratuity.' Winston didn't eat out much, not counting his trips to fast food joints, but when he did, he was always cowed into giving a ten or fifteen percent tip because he couldn't stand the accusing looks waiters gave people who didn't tip. Now, though, with the spine starch he'd received from his grandmother's handling of Leland Carter, he decided to take a stand. A ten percent service fee – for what service he did not know – was more than enough. So, he drew a firm line through 'Gratuity,' and totaled up the drink charges, tax, and service fee, and wrote that amount at the bottom of the slip, which he slid back across the counter. The bartender picked it up, looked at, glared at Winston, who glared right back, and then put the slip into the register and went back to wiping at the countertop.

Winston turned his back on the man and looked around the restaurant. Half the tables were still vacant, and he noticed three or four male waiters standing around with nothing to do. Two couples who had come in behind him and Megan were seated, and one already had salads in front of them.

Megan was sipping at her Coke, and appeared not to notice any of this, but Winston's blood pressure was elevated, and he felt a throbbing vein at the base of his neck. He put his drink on the counter and walked over to the greeter standing idly at the entrance with a look of complete indifference on his face.

"Ahem," Winston said quietly. The man ignored him. "Hmmph. Harrumph." In a louder voice.

After a noticeable pause, the man turned and looked down his nose at Winston. "Yes, is there something I can do for you?"

"Yes, as a matter of fact there is," Winston said. "I can't help but notice that there are a number of vacant tables, and that some people who came in after us are already being served."

"Of course, Sir," the man said in an icy tone. "The people who were seated have reservations. Patrons with reservations are always seated immediately. Without a reservation, you must wait until a table is cleared. You have obviously not dined here before, and are not aware of our customs."

"No, you're right, I'm not familiar with your customs," Winston said. As he spoke, he pulled out his wallet and without looking fished out a banknote. As he held it up, he noticed that it was a ten rather than a single, which he'd intended to use. "Perhaps this will help ease my way into learning how things are done here."

The man's eyebrows raised and the beginning of a smile creased his face until he got a closer look at the bill. The snotty expression returned.

"I'm not sure we can do anything for you, Sir," he said, and started to turn away.

Winston cleared his throat. "I wonder how it would look in the *Washington Post* if there was an article about a restaurant refusing to serve a customer with so many empty tables about," he said. "It might just affect that establishment's star rating, don't you think?"

Up went the eyebrows again, and his head wrinkled as he peered more closely at Winston. Then, he snatched the ten dollar bill from Winston's hand. "Well, I suppose I can do something for you. Please just wait here a moment." He spun on his heels and walked quickly toward the back. Winston noticed that the heels of his shoes were worn lopsided, and the leather was scuffed.

In less than a minute, the man was back. Following in his wake was a thin, blonde girl wearing a black skirt and a white blouse and carrying an order pad.

"If the gentleman and his companion would kindly follow Marie here, she will seat you and take your order. Bon appetite," the greeter said. He then turned back to his station at the entrance, but kept shooting worried glances Winston's way.

"This way, please," the blonde said, and walked toward the back of the room without looking back to see if Winston and Megan followed.

She walked and walked until she could walk no further. The table to which she led them was in the restaurant, but just barely. It was in the back of the room, in the darkest corner, which was lit periodically when the door to the kitchen opened. He looked at the woman, frowning deeply.

"Is this the best table you have?"

"Yes, Sir, it is," she said. "This near the kitchen, we can be sure your food's still hot when it reaches the table, and if you have any complaints, the chef doesn't have to walk far to get to you to sort things out."

Winston looked puzzled. Megan, who until now had been silent, poked him silently in the ribs. "I have a feeling they think you might be a food critic for the newspaper," she whispered in his ear. "A table near the kitchen is, I've heard, a mark of status."

Winston looked from Megan to the waitress, who stood with her order pad poised, a broad smile on her narrow face. Megan was obviously more knowledgeable about such things than he was, so he decided to take her word for it. He held the chair for her to sit, than took the chair opposite her. The waitress placed menus in front of them.

"Would you care for something to drink before you place your order?"

I don't think so. Heck, most of the lunch hour's already shot. "No, thank you," Winston said. "We'll order now if you don't mind."

She sniffed and opened her pad.

"I think I'll just have the chef's salad and an ice tea," Megan said.

It wasn't what Winston had in mind, but it would thankfully be inexpensive. "That sounds good," he said. "I think I'll have the same, only no sugar in my tea, please. Would you like sugar in yours, Megan?"

"No, I like mine without sugar as well, but with a slice of lemon." The waitress looked disappointed, but she scribbled their orders, smiled, and departed. "I'm surprised you drink your tea without sugar," Megan said after she'd gone. "Considering all the soda you drink."

Actually, Winston did like his drinks sweat. Tea was the exception. His mother always described the tea she'd seen as a child growing up in Georgia – so much sugar in it, you could see striations in the liquid, and because, for some reason, she associated sweet tea with the discrimination she'd grown up with, would never put sugar in her tea. Winston had acquired the habit from her. Coffee was different. She took hers with three spoons of sugar. Winston was a four spoon man.

"I've been thinking about losing some weight," he said. "So, I think I'll be cutting back on the sweets."

Megan looked at him pensively. "Winston, I'm sorry about this," she said. "If I'd known we needed a reservation, I would have suggested somewhere else. It's just that I'd heard such good things about it. Where do you normally eat when you eat out?"

"Oh, I usually just go to Burger King and get a fish or chicken sandwich with fries and a drink, unless I'm really hungry. Then, I get a Double Whopper with fries, a drink and a milk shake. Sometimes I go to Popeye's when I feel like chicken or Five Guys for the big bag of fries. You know . . . places like that. What about you? Where do you like to eat?"

Her look was faintly disapproving. "I bring my lunch sometimes," she said. "I don't like eating a heavy lunch. Other times I find a place like this with a varied menu, so I can eat light. I get drowsy in the afternoon if I eat a heavy lunch."

Winston was just the opposite. If he didn't eat, he got drowsy. Without food in his system he couldn't concentrate. He'd never understood how anyone could keep their mind on work when their body was crying out for food.

The waitress brought their salads and drinks, placed them on the table and quietly withdrew. They ate in silence. When they'd finished, Winston signaled for the check.

"That's okay, Sir," the waitress said. "Your meal is on the house as compensation for making you wait." She gave Winston a slight wink. "We do hope you enjoyed your meal and will remember us fondly."

Winston then realized that Megan had been right. They thought he was a food critic. *This is nice.* "I most certainly will," he said. "Especially the superb service that you have rendered."

The waitress beamed as Winston and Megan rose and departed. Outside, Megan began laughing. "Winston Nesbitt," she said, when she caught her breath. "I would have never thought you capable of such a thing."

"Actually," he said. "I've never done anything like that before in my life. It was kind of fun, though."

Megan looked at him strangely, a half smile on her brown face. They said no more during the walk back to the office building, or during the ride up in the elevator. When they got out of the elevator, she turned to him. "Thanks for lunch, Winston. I had a wonderful time." She smiled shyly at him, touched him lightly on the cheek, and ducked into her cubicle.

As he walked into his cubicle, Winston felt conflicted. On the one hand, he was happy to have spent the time with Megan. On the other, though, he felt a bit guilty for having hoodwinked the poor waitress at the restaurant. He wondered what would happen to her when no review of the place appeared in the newspaper. As he sat at his desk, he weighed the plusses and minuses. The plusses won. He *had* finally enjoyed himself. Oh, he would have liked to have had a larger lunch. The salad didn't even fill a corner of his stomach. But, he'd had that salad with Megan, and that made it worth it.

So, he finally decided that he felt good, or as close to what passed for good for him.

Charles Ray

"Boy, you better listen to your granny." – **Gran Gran**

Chapter 13

∎∎

As Winston prepared to dive into the stack of reports on his desk, his grandmother appeared in a silent flash directly before his eyes. She stood on the stack of papers he'd planned to work on, her feet apart, hands on her bony hips. Her tiny head was canted to one side, and she was frowning.

Winston had seen that frown before. It was the time she walked in on him as he sat in the bathroom playing with himself while ogled the *Sports Illustrated* swim suit issue. She hadn't said anything, she just snatched the magazine from his trembling hands and stood there, ripping it to shreds and flushing the shreds down the toilet. When the last scrap had swirled out of sight, she gave him one last glaring look and walked out, leaving him standing in the middle of the bathroom with his pants down around his ankles.

He hadn't done anything wrong this time, or at least he could think of nothing he'd done wrong. But, there she was, and there was that same accusing glare spearing through him, and making him want to confess to something, anything, just to get her to quit looking at him like that.

He could feel his crotch begin to shrink and shrivel up the same way it had done that day so long ago. *Dagnabit, why am I reacting like this? I haven't done anything wrong.* He continued to shuffle the papers, the ones that she wasn't standing on, whistling softly through his teeth, and trying to ignore her.

That never worked. His grandmother was not one to be ignored. "Even though, I wasn't there, I know your lunch was a disaster," she said. "And, don't you sit there and try to ignore me, boy."

He finally looked at her. "It wasn't all that bad," he said. He described what happened. When he got to the part where the waitress told him the meal was on the house, her glare softened.

"Okay, so that part wasn't bad. You did good. As for the rest of it, it was like getting a tooth pulled without Novocain isn't bad, like getting poked in the eye with a sharp stick isn't all that bad, like, oh, never mind." She stamped her foot. "Winston Lee Nesbitt, I told you I'd take care of finding you a proper woman, but you decided not to listen to me. You know nothing good can come of that."

He wanted to tell her to butt out, to mind her own business, but of course, he couldn't do that. She *was* after all his grandmother, and besides, he was just a little bit scared of her, even in her current tiny form. He decided to do what he'd often done as a child when she found him doing something wrong, divert her attention. He put on his most innocent look.

"Gran Gran, why is it I can see and hear you, but no one else can, and when you stamp your foot, it makes no sound?"

That had always worked when he was little. She loved to give advice and 'teach' him things. She would often become so engrossed in explaining things to him she'd forget why she originally wanted to talk to him.

"It's because I'm a spirit, you ninny," she said. "As far as I can figure, you're not really hearing my voice in your ears, but in your head. I'm not sure how it works, but trust me, it works."

That was as close as she'd ever come to admitting she didn't know something.

"Can you walk through walls and stuff like that?"

"Well, of course I . . . wait a minute. You're trying to play with me here. We were talking about your little lunch date."

Well, it had been worth a shot. "What is it about my lunch date you want to talk about?"

"I thought I told you that Little Miss

Sunshine wasn't right for you. I'm working on that," she said.

"First of all, Gran Gran, her name is Megan, and I told you already, I don't need your help in that department."

"Boy, you need my help in every department, especially that one."

"But-"

She waved her hand in a snapping motion.

"Stop sulking, boy. You know I'm just telling you the truth, and I just want what's best for you. Haven't I always given you good advice?"

"B-but, you're . . . I mean . . . how can you know what's best for me? You've been dead, uh, I mean, gone for sixteen years."

"Now, now my little Winnie Pooh," she said as she floated toward him. "Hasn't your old granny always done what was best for you? Hasn't she always been right?"

Winston had always hated it when she called him Winnie Pooh. It reminded him of soft, round fluffy creatures who were always getting stuck in impossible situations, too close to his reality for comfort.

"I know you mean well, Gran Gran," he said. "But, couldn't you give Megan a chance? Get to know her. You'll like her. She's a really nice person, and I like her a lot."

She shook her head. "I don't know. I don't think I could ever like her," she said. "You need a woman with some spunk, and the fact that she works here says she's spineless just like you. Sorry, Boy, but it's a plain fact, you got no backbone to speak of. I just don't think she's the right one for you. Now, you trust your grandma. We'll get that taken care of as soon as you get better as standing up to the pipsqueaks you work for."

Winston had never thought of Megan as being without spunk. In fact, he thought she was just about the spunkiest person he knew, certainly the spunkiest in his office. He'd never spoken to any of the other women, not in all the years he'd worked for Advantage Consulting, couldn't even remember their names, but they just didn't seem to be spunky like Megan was spunky. Of course, he'd never seen her confront Leland Carter or any of the other executives. She stayed quietly in her cubicle most of the time. But, they never picked on her either, and she always seemed to know what she was doing. On the other hand, his grandmother had, as far as he knew, always been right about things. She was the one he turned to when he had a problem. After she died, he had no one to turn to. Now, she was back. He dropped his forehead against his desk and sighed.

"Gran Gran," he murmured into the desktop. "What am I supposed to do?"

"Don't you worry, honey. You just let me take care of everything."

He sighed again. That's the way he'd done it as a child. It felt comforting to know that she was back, and he could relax and let her take care of his problems. After all, he hadn't actually done such a good job himself. She knew what to do. She always knew what to do.

Yet, a nagging doubt stirred in the back of his brain.

Chapter 14

■■■

By 4:30 Winston had finished the report he'd been working on. He decided to drop it off at Carter's office and go home. His grandmother had hovered quietly in a corner of his cubicle while he worked, and for that he was thankful.

As he shuffled the papers together and inserted them into a plastic binder, she floated higher, and drifted toward his desk, a broad smile on her face.

"Yes, Gran Gran, I'm going to see Carter. See if your treatment is still effective."

"I almost hope I have to give him another shot."

Hearing the glee in her voice, Winston almost wished the same, and then felt a twinge of shame for the thought.

As he neared Carter's office, the COO, Archibald DeMille, came out of his office which was next door. He pointed a pudgy brown finger at Winston. "Mr. Nesbitt, may I have a word with you?" he said.

Winston stopped mid-stride. He'd not had much contact with DeMille, except in the group torture sessions chaired by Carter, and he wasn't sure how to respond to him.

"Go ahead, Winston Lee. Let's see what Porky Pig wants."

Accustomed to taking orders from whoever spoke first or loudest, Winston turned and walked toward DeMille. "Yes, Sir," he said. "What can I do for you?"

DeMille stepped aside and motioned for Winston to enter his office.

"Come in, Mr. Nesbitt.," he said.

Warning bells were clanging in Winston's head. DeMille had never called him 'Mister' before. He'd always been 'Nesbitt,' or 'hey you.' He was mildly shocked, but upon entering DeMille's office for the first time, he was shocked beyond words.

Even Gran Gran was impressed.

"Well, the rich play while the poor struggle. I wonder if he ever does any work in here," she said.

Winston wasn't sure what he expected to see in the number two executive's office, but what he was seeing definitely was not it.

The floor was covered with a plush, violet carpet with bright yellow flowers embroidered in it. The desk, in the center of the room, was large, larger even than Leland Carter's desk, and made from some dark, expensive wood. It was oval shaped, and had a concave indentation in it, in which sat a large, high backed, leather executive chair. The back, seat and arms of the chair were deep black leather, worn from years of DeMille's body rubbing against it. On the walls were several expensive looking oil paintings of hunting scenes, between which hung diplomas and certificates from schools Winston had never heard of. In the center of the desk was a gold pen set that looked like it cost more than Winston's bi-weekly salary. Missing from the desk was anything, even a scrap of paper, that indicated DeMille did any work.

He maneuvered his corpulent frame around behind the desk and into the chair, leaning back and looking up at Winston. He looked like a fat brown frog.

"My goodness," Gran Gran said. *"I've seen pictures of Buckingham Palace, and the Queen of England doesn't have an office as fancy as this."*

"It is something, that's for sure," Winston thought back at her. He stood there, waiting for DeMille to offer him a seat in one of the expensive looking chairs that flanked the desk, or tell him why he was there, but the man just kept looking up at him. "Why did you want to see me, Sir," Winston finally asked. DeMille played with the gold desk set for a few seconds, then he made a noise deep in his throat and looked at Winston through narrowed eyes. "Leland tells me you did something to him," he said.

"Sir?" Winston asked innocently.

"Don't play dumb, Mr. Nesbitt. Leland said you were acting strange, and that you put some kind of hex on him."

"Well, Sir, I think Mr. Carter's been working a bit too hard, if he thinks he was hexed." Winston laughed. "How could I do anything to him? Hex? What kind of hex?" Winston pointed at the diplomas. "Surely, a man with your education doesn't believe in such stuff."

Winston's grandmother chuckled.

DeMille did not look amused. His dark face got two shades darker, and he toyed with the gold pen set. It was a long time before he could look up and meet Winston's gaze.

"Now, see here, Nesbitt," he said. "We can't have employees abusing their superiors . . . and, especially not the owner of the company. I want you to tell me what you did to Leland. I know you didn't put a hex on him, but you did *something*, and I want to know what."

"What about superiors abusing their workers?" Winston asked. DeMille's eyes went wide, and his fleshy lips quivered. "I didn't *do* anything. I was talking to Mr. Carter, and he suddenly got sick, that's all. Maybe he had an attack of guilt or something. I certainly didn't do anything to him."

Winston had his hands in his lap, below the level of the desk. He'd crossed his fingers on both hands. *I'm going to hell for that lie.*

No, baby, you are not. A lie told for a good cause won't get you punished.

Winston hoped his grandmother knew what she was talkin about. DeMille, on the other hand, still needed some convincing.

He rubbed his fleshy jaw with a fleshy hand, and fixed Winston with a skeptical glare. "Did you or did you not tell him that if he didn't apologize to you, something bad would happen to him?"

"Well, yes sir, I did," Winston said. "But, that's not putting a hex on anyone. I never touched him. I think it was his guilty conscience that made him sick. That can happen sometimes, you know."

DeMille rubbed at his jaw harder, causing it to quiver. "Just why in the world do you think he should apologize to you in the first place?"

"Mr. DeMille, you know good and well that he's always mistreating and insulting me. In fact, he's downright cruel sometimes. For that matter, so are you and Mr. Park."

"So, what next, Nesbitt? Are you planning on insisting that *we* apologize to you as well? And, if we don't, is something bad going to happen to us?" DeMille had a sneer in his voice.

Winston looked at Gran Gran. She nodded.

"As a matter of fact, yes sir, that is what I was planning to do," he said. "And a raise in pay would be nice as well."

Gran Gran gave him a thumb up and a big smile. *Now, you're learning, boy.*

DeMille's porcine eyes widened in surprise, giving his face the appearance of a large, featherless, brown owl. His fleshy lips formed a little 'O.' He shook his head. "You're joking, right? Surely you jest, man. What makes you think you deserve a raise?"

"Oh, surely I'm *not* joking," Winston said. "You, Mr. Carter and Mr. Park have been really mean to me, and the two of you should apologize just like Mr. Carter did. As for the raise, I haven't had a pay increase for over three years. I think a raise is long overdue. I do a lot of work around here, and I should get paid for it."

That's telling him, Winston Lee. I knew you had it in you, just had to poke you a little to get it to come out.

"Thank you, Gran Gran.

Now, you just go on and find something to do, child. Let me take care of this pig. You really don't want to see what I have planned for him.

In fact, he did want to see. Watching the things she could do was becoming as addictive as chocolate – not particularly good for you if you indulged too much, but oh so satisfying. But, the tone in her voice left no room for argument, so he meekly left the room.

As he was leaving, he heard his

grandmother say, *"Come here, piggy, piggy. Granny has a little surprise for you."*

He knew DeMille couldn't hear her, but he could sure feel her presence, because her voice was followed immediately by him saying, "Oomph," and then "Oh, oh my," and "Oh, no!" As the door closed behind him, Winston heard DeMille whimpering, sounding, as Carter did, like an animal in pain.

He found himself wishing his grandmother had come back earlier. She was something else.

Winston felt like whistling. As he neared his cubicle, he saw John Park peering around the door of his office. As Winston looked in his direction, Park's eyes went round in a shocked expression and he ducked back inside, pulling the door shut.

Oh yes, Winston was feeling really, really good.

Charles Ray

"He'd make a lovely corpse." – **Charles Dickens**
(*Martin Chuzzlewit*)

Chapter 15

Leland Carter greeted Winston with an obsequious smile when he delivered the finished report. There was not, however, any mirth in his eyes. Instead, there was fear. Fear and a large portion of respect. He seemed happy and relieved when Winston only put the report on his desk and withdrew without speaking.

He turned to check on DeMille and see what his grandmother had done to the man. From the direction of Park's office he heard the sound of the door being quickly closed.

He entered DeMille's office without knocking. The man was sitting splayed in his chair. His face glistened with sweat, and there were large dark rings under the arms of his jacket. He was breathing heavily through his mouth and his eyes were red. He glanced up at Winston with an imploring look.

"Ah, there you are Nes-, Mr. Nesbitt," he said as he gasped for breath. "I-I've been t-thinking, and I think p-perhaps you're right. We haven't always treated you with the respect you deserve, so on behalf of the company, please accept my sincerest apologies for any emotional distress you might have suffered. We have treated you poorly, and you have my assurance as COO that such treatment will cease forthwith, and will never happen again. Oh yes, and there will be a small increase reflected in your next paycheck."

"How small of an increase?"

DeMille's eyes blinked rapidly. He looked right and left. "Uh, would fifteen percent be sufficient?" he asked.

Fifteen percent! Winston would have been ecstatic over five. *Gran Gran must have really done a number on him.* "Fifteen percent will be fine," he said. "And, thank you for your generosity."

"Very well, then," DeMille said. "I guess that will be all then. You may go back . . . er, I mean you should return to . . . oh, whatever you wish." He waved his hands dismissively, and then caught himself and darted his gaze around the room. His lips trembled, and he looked like he wanted to cry.

Winston was tempted to say 'boo!' just to see what he'd do. Instead, he smiled, turned and walked out of the office.

As he walked away, he heard DeMille sigh loudly – almost a whimper. He had to clench his teeth to keep from laughing out loud.

Charles Ray

Chapter 16

∎∎

As good as Winston felt about getting a bump in pay, and seeing his three tormentors brought low, he would have felt a lot better if he'd been able to make a better impression on Megan. At that moment – at any moment – she meant more to him than all the money in the world.

He wished that he could convince his grandmother that Megan was the girl for him, the only girl for him. Gran Gran had some old fashioned ideas about what made a good mate, ideas that probably had gone out of style before Winston was born. The fact was, he hadn't thought that far ahead. He wanted a relationship with Megan. Then, he'd worry about what came next.

Winston had never been good around girls. In high school, because of his ineptitude, he was called, 'Casper,' 'chocolate Milquetoast,' and 'Virgin.' He'd worked up the nerve to ask a girl out only one time during the entire four years of high school; he'd asked Cindy Caldwell to go with him to the senior prom. Cindy was in the chess club with Winston, and was nearly as socially inept as he was. But, on prom night, when he showed up at her house to pick her up, she came to the door wearing an off-the-shoulder gown, and makeup that had transformed her into a vision of loveliness that caused Winston to stutter and almost stab her when he pinned on her corsage. At the dance, he'd stepped on her foot the first time they danced, and spilled red punch on her white gown right afterwards.

He was fortunate that the prom had been held in late May that year, and graduation had been just before the end of June. He'd only had to endure a month of teasing and taunting before he left high school behind.

Right after graduation, Winston enlisted in the Air Force. It was before his eighteenth birthday, so he needed a parent's permission. His mother and father seemed all too willing to agree. His father tried to talk him into joining either the Army or the Marines, arguing that either would make more of a 'man' out of him that the Air Force would, but Winston had seen the recruiting posters and the recruiters had visited his high school and talked about all the 'manly' things the soldiers and marines did, like sleeping in tents and marching through the woods for incredibly long distances, and, oh by the way, getting ready to go to war in a place called Vietnam, which he couldn't find on a map. Not that it mattered. The idea of getting shot at, even when you could shoot back, didn't appeal to him. The Air Force recruiter, on the other hand, had talked about all the training opportunities available, and the pictures he showed were all mostly indoors, with not one tent in sight. He'd dug in his heels for the first time in his life, and his father had finally given up and signed the papers.

Winston had been sent to an Air Force Base in Texas where, after basic training, he'd been trained as a personnel specialist, a title that was changed to human resources specialist shortly after he graduated. Basically, it meant that he spent his first four years in the Air Force processing promotions, leave, and other paperwork for other airmen and women in the units to which he was assigned. Except for the abortive camping trip during training, he never had to sleep in a tent or carry a weapon. He even managed to skip most of the physical training activity, except for the annual PT test that everyone had to take. He had a natural talent for paperwork, and the officers and sergeants for whom he worked appreciated that, so he managed each year to pass the PT test by one or two points – including a couple of times when he hadn't even shown up in time to take the tests.

He'd been lucky and had spent his entire

first hitch in Texas, and he was happy for it. He didn't think he'd like living overseas. For starters, he'd never been good at foreign languages, barely passing Spanish in high school, and dropping out of French after the third class. As far as he was concerned, Texas, with the drawling way people talked in many places, was as foreign as he ever wanted to experience. For a kid who'd never been more than a hundred miles from his place of birth before joining the Air Force, it was almost too foreign.

But, he'd enjoyed life in the service for the most part. Enjoyed it so much, in fact, that at the end of his first four-year hitch, he'd reenlisted for two more. He managed to get himself reassigned to Andrews Air Force Base in Prince Georges County, Maryland, just outside Washington, DC, and when his new commander learned that his parents lived only 40 miles away in Montgomery County, he'd been allowed to move in with them. He took the bus from their house to the base and back every day. As a human resources specialist for the base supply office, he didn't have to work on weekends, so it was a lot like being in school.

At the end of that term he'd planned to reenlist for another two years, but his grandmother died. His parents seemed devastated, and he didn't want to take a chance of the Air Force reassigning him somewhere outside the Washington area, so he got out.

He started looking for a job in the area so he could remain close to them, and found one with Advantage Consulting as an analyst within a week.

After more than sixteen years, he still wasn't completely sure what his job description was. He was given reports and asked to analyze them and make recommendations to clients, usually on how to save money. In many ways, it was similar to what he'd done in the Air Force, with the difference that it paid slightly more. So, day after day, he did what he was told, collected his paycheck every two weeks, and didn't complain. That was his life. Go to work five days a week, collect his check, pay his bills, spend the weekend watching TV, only to start the whole cycle over on Monday. Sometimes on weekends he would clean the house – except for the closets bulging with birthday packages. He never went out to dinner, or went for walks, and his main exercise was walking up and down the stairs.

Then, his parents, for whom he'd sacrificed a potential military career in order to stay close to, had up and moved to Florida.

His father had called him into the den the day before they left.

"Come in, Winston. Please have a seat," his father had said. Winston recognized the tone of voice. It was the one he used when he was about to tell him something he didn't want to hear, like, "Sorry, son, but you're not getting that American Flyer bike you wanted for Christmas, after all."

Winston perched on the edge of the wooden straight back chair that faced the overstuffed lounge chair in which his father spent most of his time at home, usually smoking his pipe or reading medical journals. William Edward Nesbitt was a successful proctologist with two offices, one in Rockville and one in Germantown. He had two younger physicians working for him, as well as over a dozen nurses, medical technicians, billing clerks, and assorted other employees.

When Winston was small, his father had hopes that he might follow him into the field of medicine. But, the thought of the part of the body that his father specialized in made Winston cringe. Fortunately, as he got older, it became apparent that his math and science skills were too weak to get him into medical school, and his lack of manual dexterity would have made him a danger to patients had they not. His father stopped dreaming of turning his practice over to him.

Winston leaned forward in the chair, his hands clasped together and placed atop his knees, which were also pressed tightly together. "What is it you want to talk about, Dad?" He asked with a slight tremor in his voice. He didn't know what was on his father's mind, but he knew it wouldn't be good.

William Nesbitt took his time knocking the loose ash from his briar pipe, and placing it carefully in the rack on the table at his elbow, a rack that contained five other pipes he'd picked up during his travels. His study, a room to which Winston was seldom invited, and rarely wanted to enter, was the only place where he was allowed to smoke his pipes. Even with a device that was designed to clear the smoke from the air, the smell of stale tobacco permeated the drapery and the upholstery, and Winston would have sworn, even the air. As a child, Winston had developed an allergy to smoke of any kind, and had never really gotten over it, so his father never had to tell him to stay out of his den. In fact, in order to get him into the room, he had to issue the invitation twice.

After a long pause, he turned his attention to Winston. He cleared his throat, and brought his hands together in an almost praying position at his waist. "Son, I have decided to retire and sell my practice."

Winston let his breath out. It wasn't bad news after all. "That's good news, dad. Now you can spend more time for yourself. You and mom can travel more."

His mother, the former Elizabeth Carlton Pettigrew of Atlanta, was fond of traveling so she could show off her doctor husband to people while she traveled, and show off her latest acquisitions to people when she came back home. Winston was happy for both of them, but most of all for his father who spent long hours going back and forth between his two clinics, peering up the backsides of patients from as far away as Philadelphia in order to provide the means for his wife to brag. He worked the hours he did to give her and Winston the kind of life his parents had never been able to give him when he was growing up in the hard scrabble farm country of the Texas Panhandle.

Proctology had given Winston a comfortable childhood as far as material things were concerned, and had paid his way through night school after he left the Air Force. But, he could not understand why anyone would want to practice in that particular medical field.

Thinking he'd heard what his father had called him to hear, he started to rise, but William wasn't finished. He waved Winston back down.

"Well, yes, we do plan to travel a little," he said. "But, that's not really what I wanted to talk to you about." He still had that 'you're not going to like this' tone in his voice.

Suddenly, Winston wasn't so happy any more.

"W-what did you want to talk to me about, Dad? Do I really want to hear it?"

He was sure he didn't want to hear it. He knew he wouldn't like it, whatever it was.

"Well, Winston, I don't know. I should think you'd be happy to hear it, but with you it's always hard to tell. You've always been such a sensitive person, it's hard for me to know what makes you happy and what makes you sad."

"What is it I should be happy about?"

His father leaned forward and placed a long-fingered hand, the hands of a brilliant surgeon had he so chosen, on Winston's knee. "It's like this, Winston. Your mother and I have decided that in our golden years, our old bones can no longer stand winter here in Maryland. So, I plan to sell my practice, retire, and the two of us are moving to Ft. Lauderdale, Florida. We'll leave the house to you. The mortgage is paid off, so you'll have no worries there, as long as you remember to pay the property taxes. We thought about moving to Texas, but I still have some bad memories from growing up there, and I don't think I can ever go back. Your mother talked about going back to Atlanta, but heck, in the winter it's almost as cold there as it is here, and as far as I'm concerned the social customs there are still a bit backward." He paused and leaned back in his chair. "So, after thinking about it for a long time, we decided that Florida was the best compromise."

Winston jerked back as if he'd been struck in the face. In a way, he had. How could his parents pack up and go off to Florida, leaving him all alone? It was one thing when he'd been apart from them in the

Air Force. The sergeants made all the decisions, so he never really had to. He'd never been on his own. He felt like crying, but he knew if he did that, his father would lecture him on the importance of being a man and 'bucking up,' or something along those lines. He wondered if it might be possible, though, to talk them out of it.

"Aren't you worried about hurricanes in Florida?"

"Ft. Lauderdale doesn't get hit that often," he said. "There's really nothing to worry about."

"Well, what about the fact that Florida is still in the south? You don't want to go back to Texas because of that," Winston said. "What's the difference?"

William Nesbitt sighed. "You're thinking about the northwest, or the panhandle, and even that part's not too bad because of all the northerners who've moved south to retire. And, Miami is mostly Cuban." He leaned forward. "You just don't want us to move, is that what your objections are all about?"

Winston's cheeks got warm. "W-well, yeah, I guess I don't want you guys to leave. What'll I do here all by myself?"

"Winston, you've *got* to learn to take care of yourself." The expression on his face was now one of exasperation, another one that Winston was familiar with.

"Okay, pop, if that's what the two of you really want to do, I guess I wish you the best," Winston said. He tried to put on a brave front, but at that moment he wasn't feeling too brave. "I suppose you're right, it is time I was on my own."

"I was hoping you'd see it that way, Winston. It's about time you were on your own anyway." He picked up the magazine from the table and began reading.

The meeting was over. Winston was being dismissed. He stood and walked out of the den, his shoulders slumped.

His parents were running away from home, leaving him to fend for himself. It was supposed to be the kids who ran away from home, not the parents. He wondered if they were ashamed of him, and really wanted him to leave, but didn't want to hurt his feelings by throwing him out. Moving to Florida had probably been his mother's idea. It would be like her to come up with that solution. She'd probably thought that Winston would never be able to cope with a strange environment without someone to make his decisions, so it was best if they moved and let him stay.

Despite his misgivings, Winston did okay on his own. There'd been some rough moments the first two or three years. He often forgot to do laundry, only to discover on Monday morning that he had no clean underwear. Sometimes he'd forget to take things to the dry cleaners, and he'd have to wear a rumpled suit to work. But, he always kept a good supply of beer, pretzels and various kinds of canned food. Occasionally he would forget to buy fresh vegetables and fruit, or forget that he'd bought fresh vegetables and fruit until they were wilted or had turned black or sickly gray in the bottom of the refrigerator. Early on, he'd put dirty dishes in the sink and wash them every ten days or so, or whenever he ran out of clean plates. One day, just as he was about to wash the dishes, a large, gray, icky rat crawled out from beneath the stack of plates. It paused on the edge of the sink and looked at Winston with an arrogant, insolent stare before jumping to the floor and disappearing behind the stove. Winston barely made it to the bathroom in time to throw up into the commode.

From that day on, he washed the dishes every day. He also cleaned the house at least every other day.

"I can change my own diapers." - **Winston Nesbitt**

Chapter 17

∎∎∎

For some reason, Winston didn't sleep well that night. After the events of the day, he should have been elated, and should have slept like a log. Instead, he tossed and turned all night.

He'd always had someone telling him what to do, when to do it, and how to do it. He had enjoyed seeing his grandmother give bullies a taste of their own medicine. But, having her here solving his problems, telling him what to do – in general running his life – wasn't a completely pleasant feeling. For once, for the first time that he could remember, he felt like making his own decisions.

As he stood in the bathroom, staring at his reflection in the mirror, he realized that he *could* make his own decisions. Hadn't he taken the initiative in asking Megan out? Sure, he'd let her pick the place, and that hadn't been the best choice, but he'd *asked* her out, and that was a major step for him. He'd shown himself that he could do it. Now, all he had to do was find a way to convince his grandmother that he was ready to make decisions on his own.

That, he knew, would take some doing. In life, she'd been a small, but imposing figure. She even intimidated his father, who he'd always viewed as a strong person, but he never argued or disagreed with her. His mother, who liked to think of herself as an independent person – she certainly acted that way with his father – was scared to death of her. Whenever Gran Gran was around, Winston's mother was quiet and withdrawn. He'd never understood it. Gran Gran was a tiny woman. She never raised her voice. She was given to salty language, and could be sarcastic at times, but there was nothing else about her that indicated any special power over others. Despite this, she was the center of power and control wherever she happened to be. Total strangers would defer to her, from the meter readers who would decide not to ticket his father's car whenever Gran Gran was near, to the clerks in stores, who bent over backwards to please her. When she set her mind to something, it was impossible to change it. Yet, he felt had to try.

She had, at least, kept to her promise not to greet him when he woke up by floating inches in front of his face. He loved her, but the thought of her tiny figure floating in midair before his face when he woke up creeped him out.

He somehow managed to get through his morning routine of shower, shave and get dressed. Thankfully, it was such a routine, he didn't have to think about it, because his mind was on a thousand other things, and if anyone had asked him what he was doing, they would have been met with a blank stare.

Cleaned and dressed, he went downstairs to the kitchen. She hadn't appeared in the bathroom, and she wasn't sitting in the middle of the table as he ate a solitary breakfast.

He wondered if she was still angry with him because of his act of rebellion. Or, he hoped against hope, maybe she'd decided to let him fly solo. Could she have decided to finally accept Megan?

These thoughts hovered over him during the walk to the bus stop. They nagged at him during the bus ride to the metro station. And, they were still with him as he sat on an inward facing seat on the Red Line train pulling out of the Shady Grove Metro Station, as she winked into view just off his left shoulder.

"Morning, Winston Lee. How did you sleep last night?"

"Actually, I didn't sleep very well."

Her brown face wrinkled in a look of concern. *""What's wrong? Did you eat something last night that disagreed with you?"*

"It wasn't anything I ate. It's just . . . oh, never mind. It's something I need to work out for myself."

To keep her from knowing, Winston began looking around the car at his fellow passengers. The car, as usual, was crowded with early morning commuters, each absorbed in his or her own world, and studiously ignoring everyone else. Directly across from him, however, was a young woman who glanced covertly around her as she took noisy sips from a plastic cup containing a bright red liquid. She looked to be in her early twenties, with long, dark brown hair framing what would have been an attractive face but for the disdainful look she gave him every time she caught his eye as she sucked in the red concoction. She was of that category of rider that infuriated Winston. Disdainful of the rules, and not caring about how her actions might affect her fellow passengers, she looked at the world with an expression that defied anyone to challenge her. Pretty or not, he felt that people like her deserved some kind of punishment for their selfish behavior.

The way his grandmother's thin lips curled down, it was obvious that she felt the same.

"You want me to do something about that, Winston Lee?"

As much as he wanted to be able to handle things himself, Winston very much wanted his grandmother to do something. Aside from people who insisted on jamming their oversized bodies into a seat that had insufficient room, Winston particularly disliked the people who blatantly ignored the signs in the stations and cars that said eating and drinking was prohibited. One didn't even have to be literate to know what they said, because they also included pictures of a sandwich and a glass with the universal 'prohibited' slash through them. Oh yes, he would like her to do something about it. It might make him feel better.

"Yes, Gran Gran, please do something about it."

"I thought you'd never ask."

She chuckled. She clenched her eyes shut and wrinkled her nose. Then, she waved her right hand in the air, making a figure eight.

As Winston looked away from his grandmother to the girl opposite him, he saw her eyes widen in shock. His gaze drifted downward, and he saw the reason for her shock.

A small hole had appeared in the side of

the cup, and a jet of the bright red liquid fountained out and onto her white sweater, creating a large and growing pink circle from the top of her breasts to her waist. Her hands spasmed upwards, splashing some of the red concoction on her face and in her hair.

She squealed and muttered some words that Winston would never use, not even in private, much less in a crowded subway car. She flailed at the widening pink stain on her sweater, dropping the cup and sending the remainder of her drink down the front of her beige skirt and onto the carpet.

Winston sat there, impassively looking at the once smug face. Now, with red droplets speckling her cheeks, and her sweater and skirt ruined, she had the crestfallen look of someone whose world has come to a precipitous end. He did feel a little better, knowing she'd gotten what she deserved – but, only a little better. He noticed the other passengers briefly looking away from their papers, books, knitting or daydreaming, to gloat at her discomfiture. Misery loves an audience, he thought.

"Do you feel better, Winston Lee?"

"Yes, Gran Gran, I feel a little better."

She floated around until she was directly in front of him. She peered into his eyes, an enigmatic expression on her face. She opened her mouth, and then snapped it shut. Floating like a thistle in a mild breeze, she returned to a position near his shoulder.

Winston kept an eye on her out of his peripheral vision, wondering what was on her mind.

Charles Ray

Chapter 18

When he arrived at his office, as he was about to settle himself in his cubicle, Winston realized that there *was* one other thing he needed his grandmother to do for him.

Carter and DeMille, after sessions with her, had changed the way they dealt with him. While not exactly respectful, they no longer taunted him. John Park, on the other hand, avoided him, but whenever Winston looked at him, the Korean was staring at him with a malevolent glare. It gave Winston shivers thinking about what the man might be planning.

She was hovering in the air at the corner of his desk, looking at the calendar on his wall.

"Gran Gran, I need you to do something for me."

She swiveled around, looking him directly in the eye. *"So, you're ready to admit you need me?"*

"Uh, I've always needed you . . . why would you think I don't?"

"You know. You're trying not to think about it, but I can see it on your face. You're still smitten with that . . . oh, you know what I mean."

Winston affected a look of innocence. "Why, Gran Gran, whatever could you mean? I just need you to take care of one more little work-related issue . . . please."

She planted her hands on her hips and pursed her lips. Then, her expression softened. "Oh, hell fire, I can't stay mad at you. What do you want me to do?"

"It's Mr. Park, Gran Gran. I'm worried he might be up to no good."

She rubbed her hands together and smiled broadly. "Well, what are we waiting for? Let's pay him a visit."

Winston stood and left his cubicle. The walk to Park's office was short. He stopped at the door. Should I knock, or should I just go in?

"Just go on in, Winston Lee."

Of course, Gran Gran was right, he thought. He didn't have any contact with John Park during the normal course of business, only the torture sessions, which Winston was convinced the man sat in on just for pleasure. He pushed the door open and walked in.

Park was seated behind his desk, flipping through a large binder. At the sound of his door opening he looked up. His almond-shaped eyes widened, at first in surprise, then his thin lips turned down.

"Mr. Nesbit-u," he said. "What you come in my office-u for? I did not send-u for you."

"I'm here because we need to talk," Winston said. "And, you can cut the crap. I know you speak English as well as I do. Why do you insist on that stupid stereotyped accent?"

Winston sat in the single visitor's chair that Park kept to the right side of his desk. Park leaned back in his chair and pushed the binder to the side, frowning deeply at Winston.

"*Mr. Nesbitt*, where do you get off coming into my office and making such remarks to me?"

Winston leaned forward and stabbed a pudgy finger at the desktop.

"*Mr. Park*, you and your colleagues have been making such remarks to me, at me, and about me, from the first day I came to work here," he said. "It's time for a taste of your own medicine." Park recoiled as if he'd been struck. His cheeks darkened. "Mr. Carter and Mr. DeMille have finally come to their senses. Now, it's time for you to do the same."

"Yes," Park said. "I understand Leland has decided to give you a raise in pay. As CEO, that is his decision, of course, although I don't think you deserve it."

"You don't think I do good work for this

company?"

Park laughed. "You were hired to do a job, and you do it. If you don't do good work, you get fired. If you do good work, you continue to get paid."

"You're making no sense at all," Winston said, shaking his head. "If someone does good work, they should be rewarded for it."

Park snorted out a laugh, and made a throat clearing sound. "Your reward is being allowed to keep your job," he said. "Now, would you please remove yourself from my office?"

"Not before you apologize for the way you've treated me in the past, and promise never to do it again."

"I don't think so."

"Let me at him," Gran Gran said. She growled deep in her throat.

"Let's give him a chance first." Winston leaned closer. "Look, your colleagues reacted the same way at first, but as I told them, if you refuse to do the right thing, you will suffer for it."

"Hah! I don't know what you did to them," Park said. "But, it won't work on me. You think just because I'm Korean I'm superstitious, well I'm not, so there."

Winston leaned back in his chair and folded his arms across his chest. "No, I don't think you're superstitious. But, you need to know that I'm not the type to lie or joke. If I say something bad will happen, it will, trust me."

Park sneered and muttered something in Korean. "Okay, Nesbitt," he said. "Bring it on, because I'm not apologizing to you, not in a million years."

"Okay, Gran Gran, you heard him. I gave him a chance and he turned it down, so do your stuff." He pointed a pudgy finger at Park. "I warned you," he said. "Now it's on your head."

"You might want to leave, Winston Lee."

"No, Gran Gran, I want to see this. Besides, I think I should be here to describe what's happening to him."

"Okay, here goes."

She floated across the desk and hovered in front of John Park's face. She stared into his eyes, concentrating hard. Then, she smiled and waved both hands in the air.

Beads of sweat broke out on Park's broad forehead, on his flat cheeks, and his chin. He blinked and rubbed at his chin, staring at his moist fingertips. Then, he twitched and rubbed at his armpit. His coat showed a dark moon shape under his arms, and his palms glistened with moisture. He began to look uncomfortable.

"What are you doing to him, Gran Gran?"

"I took a look inside that pointy head of his to see what really bothers him. Would you believe it? He hates to sweat."

Park squirmed in his chair. His coat and shirt were plastered to his body now, and dark stains were appearing on the seat and legs of his trousers. His expression was pained.

"What is happening?" he asked plaintively.

"Just like I promised," Winston said. "You refused to apologize, and now you're suffering."

Gran Gran floated closer to Park, scrunching up her eyes. She bobbed her head up and down, smiling broadly. *"My, my, isn't that interesting?"* she said. She raised her right hand, finger pointing, and traced some figures in the air, then pointed downward to an area below Park's waist.

There was an immediate sound like the ripping of a sheet. A sour odor like dirty gym shoes and garlic filled the air. The ripping sound continued, and the odor became stronger. Tears filled Park's eyes.

"Jesus H. Christ," he said. "What the hell's happening to me? Nesbitt, are you doing this?"

"No, but I can make it stop. Or, more accurately, if you apologize, it will stop."

Park was breathing hard, but he pinched his nostrils together against the foul odor wafting up from his chair. Rivulets of sweat flowed down his face. "Okay, okay," he cried. "I apologize. Just make it stop."

"You promise you'll never abuse me again?"

"Yes, yes," he said. "I promise. Now,

please, make it stop."

Winston nodded at Gran Gran. She snapped her fingers. The odor disappeared. The sweat dried up. Park's clothes were suddenly dry. He sat back in his chair with a dazed expression. "How did you do that?"

"I didn't do anything," Winston said. "But, if you renege on your promise, I can see that it happens again."

"It won't, I promise," Park said. "Now, please go away and leave me alone."

Winston rose and, laughing, he went back to his cubicle.

Charles Ray

Chapter 19

∎∎∎

Back in his cubicle, with another file open on his desk, Winston reflected on what had happened. He was feeling a lot better now, and he had to confess, it was *fun* having his grandmother and her abilities around. After leaving Park's office, she'd disappeared – off again to wherever it was she went when he couldn't see her.

He was just about to start a rewrite of a report that, for a change, he'd decided himself needed more work, when Megan peeked around the edge of his cubicle entrance.

"Hi, Winston," she said. "Can I talk to you?"

"Uh, sure, Megan," he said, turning to look up at her. "What do you want to talk about?"

She walked in, moved a stack of papers from his extra chair and sat down. "It's about . . . our lunch date."

Winston blushed. If his complexion had been lighter, she would have seen. But, he felt it – the hot flush of his cheeks. "G-gosh, Megan, I'm really sorry about that."

She reached across the desk and laid a hand on his. Her hand felt warm and smooth. His breath caught in his throat.

"No, Winston, I'm the one who should be apologizing," she said. "You see, I was so happy that you'd asked me out, and I wanted our first date to be special. I wanted to impress you by picking what I thought would be a sophisticated place. I didn't know it would turn out to be a four-star wannabe. It was a disaster, and it's all my fault."

He looked at her and blinked. He shook his head. He couldn't believe what he was hearing. Things didn't go well, and someone else was taking responsibility for it. He took three deep breaths.

"Yeah, it really was a pretty lousy place, wasn't it?" Where had *that* come from? Winston Nesbitt had never been good at smart quips. "Funny thing, though, I didn't notice it at the time."

"How could you miss it? It was all pretense and no service until they thought you were a food critic."

"I guess I was so busy looking at you, and how nice you looked," he said.

Spots of color blossomed on her cheeks. "R-really, Winston? You think I look nice?"

"Of course I do. And, next time maybe we

can go to a place that's short on pretentiousness and long on service . . . something that befits a woman like you."

"Then, you forgive me?"

Now it was his turn to pat her hand. "Megan, there's nothing to forgive," he said. "I could never be angry with you, don't you know that?"

"Oh, Winston, you're such a sweetheart. That's why I lo-, er, like you so much." She squeezed his hand.

"Gosh, I like you too."

He felt as if he was floating somewhere up near the ceiling looking down on what was happening. This was definitely not him doing and saying these things.

She stood and leaned forward, kissing him lightly on the cheek. It made him feel giddy, like maybe he was going to faint. He sat there for a long time after she left, with a goofy expression on his face. Then he shook himself and went back to work. He worked for the rest of the afternoon on autopilot, completely unaware of the content of the documents he shuffled back and forth, and not caring. He felt like it was Christmas, and he *had* received that American Flyer bike he wanted.

Charles Ray

"That's it, grandma, you're outta here." - **Winston Nesbitt**

Chapter 20

■ ■

Winston made up his mind. He would have to confront his grandmother about the question of his love life.

It surprised him that he would be thinking in terms of a 'love life' where Megan was concerned, but he'd felt a warmth in her kiss that still caused a tingling feeling in his spine even hours after the fact.

He would have to make his grandmother see that his feelings for Megan were real, and that she apparently felt the same. He finally had the courage to face the fact that he was in love with Megan; madly, totally in love with her, and even if it meant making his grandmother angry, he was intent on pursuing that love. If she was angry, he'd just have to love with it. Since she wasn't technically alive, she couldn't exactly *live* with it, so she'd have to do whatever it was that spirits did in such situations. On this one, though, Winston was prepared to be as stubborn as she was.

He thought it strange that she didn't appear even once during his subway and bus ride home. She'd seem to enjoy putting unruly passengers in their places.

When he arrived home, as he was hanging his jacket in the front hall closet, he noticed a flickering out of the corner of his eye.

Gran Gran was in the living room, floating in front of the fireplace. A small flame flickered on one of the logs that had been in the hearth since the end of winter. She pointed a finger at the log, causing the flame to flare up, and then she floated up toward the vaulted ceiling. She was surrounded by an aura that flickered like a candle in a breeze. As she neared the ceiling, she paused, and then swooped down to within inches of the floor.

Winston walked softly into the living room, stopping just behind the leather sofa that faced the fireplace. He looked on as she performed her acrobatic and pyrotechnic maneuver several more times, adding loops and barrel rolls as she dove downward.

Finally, she came to a stop, a few inches above the floor. She turned around to face him, looking up at him with a glint of mischief in her eyes. He stood there silent, waiting for her to speak. His nerves twitched.

When she spoke, her voice was soft. "Well, Winston Lee, what have you been up to?" Despite the softness, there was a hint of anger in her voice.

It was time for the confrontation. Winston knew it was inevitable, and would get no easier by being put off. He'd seen, though, what she did to the people on the subway, and to his bosses. He wondered if she'd do the same to him, favorite grandson or not. He would have to find out sooner or later.

"Not much, grandma," he said. Her brows twitched. He'd never addressed her as 'grandma' before. "Just work and stuff." *Damn, I sound like a kid who just got caught up to his shoulder in the cookie jar.*

"You were with that woman, weren't you?"

Her eyes glinted. Winston shook inside, but for the first time in his life, it wasn't fear that made him shake, it was anger.

"Grandma. She. Is. Not. That. Woman," he said, shaking with fury. "If you can't remember her name, must ask me. It's Megan. Megan, not *that woman.* Can't you understand that?"

He exhaled. It felt as if a great weight had

been lifted from his shoulders.

His grandmother swooped away from him, then back toward the fireplace. She had a confused look on her face.

"Baby, hasn't grandma always done what's right for you?" Her face, at first red with anger, softened a bit. "Why, don't you remember the time I caught you playing with your little winkie?"

"Playing with my what?"

"Oh, come on, Winston. Even you can't be that dense. You remember, the time in the bathroom? The girlie magazine-"

"Gran Gran!" His cheeks felt white hot. "How could you?"

"How could *I*? I wasn't the one doing anything, it was you."

"Gran Gran, *please.*"

"Okay, okay. But, I just wanted to remind you, that I didn't tell your parents, and I didn't spank you. I didn't yell at you. I just took the magazine and threw it away. I kept your little secret, too. All I've ever done is what I thought was best for you."

"I know, Gran Gran," he said. "I know you mean well, and that you want what you think's best for me. But, frankly, I think that I'm the best one to decide what's best for me in this case, and I think Megan's what's best for me. And, in this, I think what I think should be more important. After all, it is my life we're talking about."

"Well, if that's the way you must have it,

that's the way it'll be. I can't help you anymore, and it's clear that I'm not welcome around here, so I'll just leave."

That wasn't quite what he had in mind. He didn't really want her to go away, just let him make some of his own decisions. It was one thing to do everything for him when he was young, but he was not forty, and he needed to make his own way. If only he could make her see that.

"Gran Gran, you don't understand," he said. "That's not what I meant at all. Look, I do appreciate all that you've done for me, really I do. I just want you to like Megan. I like her, I like her a lot. She's important to me, and-"

"No, Winston Lee," she cut him off. "You have to choose between us, and it seems obvious that you've chosen her. So, I guess I'll have to go."

There was a little flash, and she was gone. The weight that had lifted off his shoulders came back and centered itself on his chest. He wanted to cry, but decided that he was too grown up to cry. Grown men don't cry.

He sat down in the big chair in front of the fireplace and gazed into the dying flame – and cried.

Charles Ray

Chapter 21

The next morning, Winston was still feeling bad about his grandmother leaving. He opened his eyes slowly, peering around, almost hoping she'd be floating a few inches from his face, but there was nothing there but a few dust motes.

While he shaved and brushed his teeth, he kept looking the mirror to see if she'd pop back into view perched on his shoulder with an impish grin on his face, telling him it had all been a joke, and she was just having him on. No such luck.

On the Red Line train to Chinatown, he

missed having her hovering there near his left shoulder making mental comments about the other riders. He missed her, and he was angry with himself for chasing her away. He'd chased her away just like he'd chased his parents away. Sooner or later, everyone left him.

And, she'd only wanted to help. She meant well, she always meant well, and heaven knew, he needed all the help he could get.

In time, if he'd kept his big mouth shut, maybe she would have come to like Megan.

He was in a foul mood. When a very overweight lady made as if to squeeze her body into the space next to him, he gave her a look that sent her scurrying to the back of the car. A young man with a silver ring in his nose, and two gold rings in each eyebrow, started to take a drink from a large plastic cup. The glare Winston shot his way caused him to decide against it. He put the container back into the backpack at his feet and occupied his time reading the advertising placards above the windows.

By the time he arrived at the lobby of his building, he was in what his grandmother would have called a high dudgeon. He was in no mood for rudeness, nor was he going to spend the day being ignored, not by anyone.

When he entered the lobby, he marched to the security counter, holding his identification badge up so it could be seen clearly.

As he usually did, the guard, a middle age, slightly pudgy black man with more gray than black in his hair, glanced at it with an air of indifference, nodded and tilted his head in the direction of the elevator, before turning his attention back to the *Washington Post* he had spread out on the counter.

"Ahem," Winston said. "Do you even *know* my name? Because, you hardly even looked at my ID, and I don't believe you could have read it from such a cursory glance."

The guard slowly folded his newspaper and leaned forward. His dark brown eyes regarded Winston as if he'd just walked through fresh dog poop and forgotten to wipe his feet before entering. "Of course I know your name," he said. "You're Mr. Nesbitt, and you work up for Advantage Consulting. I know every single person who works in this building. I been working here for 25 years, and I don't never forget a face or name."

Winston recoiled as if struck. "Oh. I . . . well, I 've been coming through this lobby for sixteen years, and never once have you ever said good morning, or given any kind of greeting. You know my name, but you've never said anything."

The guard sat back in the high chair and folded his arms across his chest.

"Like I said, Mr. Nesbitt," he said. "I been working here for 25 years. When I first started working here, I greeted everybody who come through that door." He leaned forward, his dark eyes angry. "But, you know what. Nobody ever said hello back. I got tired of them being so busy thinking about their important stuff and ignoring me like I was just a piece of furniture. The only time anybody ever said anything was to complain. So, I just started ignoring them back. You know what? Nobody ever noticed when I stopped saying hello. You the first person to say anything."

Winston felt like a fool. "I . . . uh, gosh . . . I'm sorry, Mister, er . . ."

"See, you don't even know my name. It's Alexander, Dennis Alexander, just like it says on the name tag here below my badge." He leaned forward. "But, nobody ever bothered to look long enough to read it."

"Gosh, Mr. Alexander, I'm really sorry. I wasn't thinking. I know how you feel about being ignored and all. I guess I was just taking it out on you because people treat me the same way."

The guard waved dismissively. "Don't worry about, and you can call me Dennis."

"Okay, Dennis, and I'm Winston, but then, you already know that, right?"

"Of course I do. Winston. Now, that's a good name. It means 'friend's settlement' or town, a good strong name. I had a cousin named Winston. He was a real character." He laughed. "I know a lot of what goes on in this building. For instance, I know you kind of sweet on that Miss Berman." He winked. "And, I think she's kinda sweet on you, too."

"Uh, er, guh . . ." was all that Winston could say at first. He hadn't realized that his feelings for Megan were so obvious that even the lobby guard noticed. "Hey, you really think she likes me?"

"No doubt about it. You just have to see the way she looks at you to know that. By the way, I hope you told her how you feel about her."

"Well, uh, ah . . . I mean . . . well, actually, I haven't," Winston was finally able to get out.

"Man, that's a big mistake. Women always need to know how you feel about 'em. They like to hear it," he said, wagging his finger at Winston. "Don't leave her wondering. Now, you take my wife, for instance, if I don't tell her I love her at least twice a week, she gets real peevish. And, when that woman gets peevish, life ain't pleasant, let me tell you."

"Really?"

"Really. We been married thirty years, and like I said, she still like to hear me say it as much as she did when we was courting. So, what I recommend is that you march right up to Miss Berman and tell her how you feel."

Winston smiled. His dark mood was considerably lightened. "Why, I believe I'll do just that. Thank you, Dennis."

"While you're at it, you might also want to tell her about that little spirit I been seeing perched on your shoulder. That's one tough looking old broad, and she got a right to know about her."

Winston took a step back, his eyes wide. "Y-you've seen a figure on my shoulder?"

"Sure, I seen her," he said. "Salty mouthed old broad, too. She wouldn't by any chance be a relative, would she – like a grandmother or an old aunt?"

"S-she's my grandmother," Winston said. "She died about sixteen years ago, and then a few days ago, she just sort of popped back into my life."

The guard smiled. "Yeah, spirits can be like that. They do come and go at odd times, especially grandmothers. The world wouldn't work without grandmothers. Seems they feel like they have to take care of things even after they dead and gone, so they come back to do it. You ought to tell that gal of yours, though, so she's not surprised if grandma pops in on your honeymoon or something." He winked at Winston.

Winston blushed again, and tried not to think about what the guard meant by 'or something.' "I suppose you're right," he said. "But, how is it you can see her when no one else can?"

"Well, down in East Texas where I come from spirits, haints, and ghosts are pretty common. Most of the time they're pretty harmless, but sometimes they can be bad. It seems it's always somebody who had some unfinished business when they died. You know what that might be in your grandmother's case?"

Winston shook his head. "No, I was away when she died, in the Air Force. I don't know what she might have wanted to do and didn't get to."

He felt a certain kinship with the guard, but not enough to share that his grandmother had come back to put *his* life right. The guard smiled and sat back on his chair.

"Well, I think it might be a good idea for you to find out, might save you a peck of trouble in the long run."

He unfolded his newspaper, and with a smile at Winston, resumed reading.

Darn it, Winston thought, *I should have talked to him long before now.*

"It's do-or-die time, but since I might die, I think I'll just wait." – **Winston Nesbitt**

Chapter 22
■■■

Winston rode the elevator up to his floor in a daze. His mind struggled to process the conversation he'd had with the lobby guard.

His grandmother's unfinished business was to run his business. He wondered how he would tell Megan about her, and if she'd think him crazy when he did. Deep down, he almost wished things would go back to the way they'd been before his grandmother appeared in his bathroom mirror. Life then was boring, but it was a predictable boring. Now, every day, every minute, was bringing something new, and he wasn't sure he could cope.

As he came out of the elevator, he bumped into one of his problems.

Megan was passing the elevator with a stack of papers in her arms, and Winston walked full tilt into her, sending the papers flying in every direction. He grabbed her arm to keep her from being knocked to the floor.

"Oh gosh, Megan," he said. "I'm so sorry. I didn't see you."

She smiled up at him, an angelic smile that caused his heart to beat faster. "Winston, I don't know whether to be flattered or insulted," she said. "I'm either so petite, you missed me, or so unremarkable, you didn't notice me."

It took him a second or two to realize that she was joking. "Megan, you are a lot of things, but unremarkable is not one of them. In fact, you're one of the most remarkable people I know, and I notice you all the time."

Her light brown cheeks turned red, and her smile turned up a couple hundred watts. "Oh, Winston, do you really mean that? Does that mean you like me?"

Ignoring the fact that every ear in the office was tuned in to their conversation, Winston said, "Megan, I more than *like* you."

As soon as the words were out of his mouth, he found himself gulping. He couldn't believe he'd had the nerve to say what he'd just said. But, he realized, he meant it. It was something he should have said long before. He puffed his chest out and smiled. Megan clasped his wrist and gazed into his eyes.

"Winston, are you saying what I think you're saying? Are you trying to tell me that you . . ."

"I love you, Megan Berman," he said. "There, I said it. What do you think of that?"

She draped her arms around his neck, pulled his head down, and kissed him on the lips. His lips at first stayed together, but under her gentle probing, they slowly parted, and for the first time in his life, Winston felt a woman's tongue in his mouth. He'd often heard the guys in high school talk about 'the tongue,' and now he knew what they were so excited about.

As Megan pulled back, all Winston could do was stand there, looking dumb, with his arms around her waist. He was in a daze, and barely heard the cheering and applause that erupted from every cubicle on the floor.

"Way to go," someone shouted.

"About time you two got it out in the open," someone else said.

"You the man, Winston," the guy from the mail room said.

"I'm so happy for you, Megan," a thin blonde girl who had a cubicle three down from Winston said.

People Winston had worked with for years, who had never done more than nod at him, and whose names he could not recall, came up to clap him on the back and shake his hand, and hug Megan. He'd seen it before, but this was his first time taking part in the back-slapping, high-fiving, well-wishing ritual, and it was fun.

A swarthy Indian man who worked in

the company's computer department placed his hands on Winston's shoulders. "You know, we have been taking bets on how long it would take for you two to finally admit you had a thing for each other. I won the lottery. Thanks."

"Yeah," the redheaded receptionist said. "You two have been making goo goo eyes for years, circling each other like two love birds afraid to land. I lost the lottery, but I'm still happy for you."

Winston and Megan stood in front of the elevator, smiling broadly. Megan took the hugs and congratulations in stride, engaging her coworkers in small talk, while all Winston could do was stand there, smiling broadly and looking dazed.

Several people shook his hand and congratulated him. Even Leland Carter came out of his office and walked up to Winston and clapped him on the shoulder.

"Darn good move, Winston," he said. "You two make a fine couple, and, I might add, two of our finest employees."

There was a sincere tone in his voice that Winston had never heard before. *Thank you, Gran Gran, wherever you are.*

Chapter 23

For Winston, the rest of the day went by in a blur.

At the close of business, he went to Megan's cubicle and asked her to have dinner with him, at his house. She accepted without hesitation, and they took the elevator down together.

As they passed through the lobby, holding hands, the guard smiled and, when Megan was distracted, winked and gave Winston a thumb-up sign. Winston smiled back and mouthed "Thanks." He walked out into the street with his head held high and feeling like his feet weren't even touching the sidewalk.

The commute was uneventful, or at least Winston noticed nothing. He was only aware of the warmth of Megan's body next to him on the train and on the bus. From the bus stop to the house, he felt again like he was walking on air. His mouth was dry, his hands trembled, and he could feel his heart pounding in his chest.

In the foyer, he took her light jacket and hung it with his coat in the hall closet. He then turned to her and took her hands in his.

"Megan, before I get dinner started," he said. "There's something I have to tell you."

She smiled up at him. "Are you going to tell me you don't know how to cook, and we'll be eating TV dinners?"

"No, no, nothing like that. I'm actually a pretty good cook. I've been cooking for myself ever since my parents moved to Florida."

"Winston, I'm just joking," she said. "Besides, I'm not really hungry, so there's no rush to eat. What do you want to tell me?"

He took her hand and led her to the living room to the large sofa in front of the fireplace. After she sat, he sat next to her, his knees touching hers, and still holding her hands.

He cleared his throat. "Megan, you might have noticed that I've been acting a bit strange the past few days."

"Strange? Strange in what way, Winston?"

"Oh, you know, just strange. Not the way I usually act."

"Well, I have noticed that you're more assertive. I mean, asking me to lunch, and then inviting me to dinner – oh yes, and telling me you love me in front of the whole office. That's not like you at all. I like it, in fact, I've been wanting you to ask me out for a long time. I'm surprised that you finally did. Happy, but surprised. Is that what you mean?"

"I've been wanting to ask you out for a long time," he said. "I guess that is strange, but it's not what I'm talking about when I say strange.

"Okay, I'm all ears. What other strange things have you done lately?

"Uh, you might have noticed me talking to myself." She nodded. "Well, I wasn't actually talking to myself. I was talking to my grandmother."

"Your grandmother? Didn't your grandmother die several years ago?"

"It's . . . well, it's actually her spirit, or her . . . ghost I've been talking to." He quickly went on to explain everything, starting with his grandmother appearing in the mirror when he was shaving.

"You poor thing," she said when he'd finished. "That must be exhausting. Is there anything I can do to help?"

"You mean, you believe me?" He looked at her with his eyes wide.

Before she could answer, there was a flash followed by a twinkle, and Gran Gran was there floating in the air a few feet in front of them.

"So, you ignored my advice and are still seeing her, I see." She fixed Winston with her most severe expression.

"Why shouldn't he see me?" Megan asked.

Winston's mouth opened in an 'O.' Gran Gran swooped backwards until she met the brick of the fireplace, her eyes wide in surprise.

"Y-you can hear her?" Winston asked.

"Y-you can see me?" Gran Gran asked.

"And, hear you too," Megan said. She turned to Winston. "Your grandmother doesn't seem to like me for some reason."

"All's well that ends well, especially when it wasn't going all that well." – **Winston Nesbitt**

Chapter 24
■■■

Gran Gran's mouth opened and closed like a fish gasping for air at the bottom of a boat. Little strangling sounds came from her tiny throat, and her eyes got all round and goggly.

Winston sat there on the sofa, his eyes round, his head swiveling from Megan to his grandmother.

Megan sat primly, gazing steadily at Gran Gran.

Gran Gran finally regained her composure. She floated over to hover a foot from Megan's face. "It's not that I don't like you, girlie," she said. "It's just that I'm not sure you're right for my little Winston."

Megan matched her stare. "First of all, I'm not girlie! My name is Megan. And, second, Winston is not your *little* anything. He's a grown man entitled to make his own decisions, and it's about time people started recognizing that. Most importantly, it's time *you* started recognizing that."

Gran Gran did a bit of the fish gasping for air with her mouth again, then she laughed, a high cackling laugh. "Well, well, girl, er, Megan," she said. "You do have grit, I'll give you that. But, dead or not, I'm still Winston's flesh and blood, or *was* his flesh and blood . . . well, you know what I mean. I only have his best interests at heart."

"So do I," Megan said. She folder her arms under her small breasts and glared at Gran Gran.

"I guess we both want what's best for him," Gran Gran said. "So, what do you suggest we do about it?"

Megan turned and looked at Winston.

"I suggest we let him decide," she said.

"Well," Gran Gran said. "That's not a bad idea. Not a bad idea at all." She swiveled in the air, looking at Winston.

Winston looked from one to the other. It wasn't really fair, asking him to choose between them. How on earth was he supposed to do that?

"Winston Lee, who was it changed your diapers when you were little and your mother didn't have time? You know how much that daughter of mine hated messy diapers? Whenever you went, she went."

"Well, Gran Gran, I guess it must have been you," he said. "Of course, I was pretty small at the time, and I really don't remember."

"Don't be playing games, Boy," Gran Gran said. "You know what I'm talking about. Who is it has been there for you whenever you needed help? How many times did I bail you out of trouble when you were growing up?"

"I know, I know," he said. "But, Gran Gran, this is not about when I was little. In case you haven't noticed, I'm not a little boy anymore, and I don't need my diapers changed."

"You tell her, Winston," Megan said.

"Keep out of this, girl, er, Megan," Gran Gran said. "This is between me and my grandson, and doesn't concern you."

"Oh, but it does," Megan said. "I think it concerns me very much, in fact."

"Hah, in a pig's eye it does."

"In a pig's eye, in a gnat's eye," Megan said, pointing her finger at Gran Gran. "You can put it anyway you want to, but Winston is now a full grown man, and when a man grows up, he has to make his own decisions."

"Now, hon, that just proves you don't know diddly squat. My little Winston ain't the kind for making decisions. He was always more comfortable letting someone else make them for him."

"I know more than you think I know. I believe I have more faith in Winston than you do. I know he can be decisive when it's really important. Maybe that's the problem . . . too many *other* people always stepping in to make his decisions for him, and he's just too polite to tell them to buzz off. It's no wonder he's so indecisive, he's never been allowed to decide anything for himself."

"As much as I hate to admit it, Megan," Gran Gran said in a voice that was now soft and reasonable. "I think you might be right. It's true that when he was little and had a problem instead of letting him figure it out for himself, someone – usually me – would step in and handle it for him."

Winston had been sitting quietly, watching the conversation, but he knew he would have to act. He also knew that whatever he decided, there was going to be one upset woman in the room afterwards.

He closed his eyes and took a deep breath.

"Grandmother," he said. "I love you dearly. B-but, I also love Megan."

"You do? Well, of course you do. I knew that from that kiss this morning." Megan looked at him smiling triumphantly.

"You do?" Gran Gran asked. She looked strange.

"I do, I really do," he said. "I've loved her since the first day I laid eyes on her; I was just too stupid and scared to tell her."

Megan grinned. "You don't know how long I waited to hear him say that."

"I've been waiting a bit myself," Gran Gran said.

"Wha- what?" asked Winston.

"What?" asked Megan.

"I wasn't exactly sure when I first came back, but I finally figured out how I was supposed to help you."

Megan looked wide-eyed at Gran Gran and snapped her finger. "You were supposed to get him to start making up his own mind and standing up for himself . . . even against you," she said.

Gran Gran beamed back at her. "That's right. You know, you're pretty smart. And, you're stubborn too. Just what my Winston needs."

Winston looked astonished. "You mean, you don't object to Megan and I being together?"

"Of course not, Boy," she said. "I just had to make sure that's what you really wanted. You had to finally make a decision for yourself, You stood up to me and defended the woman you love, but even more important, you got up the nerve to tell her how you feel about her. I'd say you're gonna be okay from here on in. Especially with her to look out for you."

Could it be that simple, he thought.

"Trust me," Gran Gran said. "It's just that simple. You decide what you want, and you stand up for it. That was something I forgot to teach you when you were growing up. I'm sorry about that, but at least I had a chance to correct that mistake." She flew around the room. "But, I also learned something else. Teaching you to make decisions wasn't the real problem I had to solve. I had to learn how to get out of the way and let you learn by yourself and make your own decisions. I made the same mistake with your mama when she was growing up."

She looked up at the ceiling. "Okay, I guess that's my next job, right?"

"What?" Winston asked.

"Oh, nothing," she said. "Just a message from . . . oh, never mind. You wouldn't understand, and it's too hard to explain. The point is, I'm proud of you, and I wish you two the best."

"Wow," was all Winston could say.

"Wow is right," said Megan. "This has been quite a day." She turned to Gran Gran. "I guess now that your unresolved issue has been taken care of, you'll be crossing over?"

"Does this mean I'll never see you again, Gran Gran?" Winston asked.

"What's the matter? You two trying to get rid of me?"

"No," he said. "I kind of got used to having you around."

"Well, you'll be happy to know that it doesn't work like that. I'm not a ghost looking to cross over. I'm a spirit, and I can go back and forth, so I'll be around from time to time. I have a few other places I have to go, and a few other things to take care of, but you don't get rid of me that easily."

"I don't mind having you around," Megan said. "I think I'd like it in fact – from time to time."

Gran Gran laughed. "Yes, of course. I would only come when needed, or if you invited me. I'll try not to drop in without notice too much. Now that I see Winston Lee's in such good hands, there's not much for me to do here. I might spend some time riding the Metro. I never rode it when I was alive, but it's kind of interesting. I can have lots of fun riding the subway."

She and Winston began laughing. Megan looked puzzled.

"Don't worry," Winston said. "I'll explain it later."

"Well, children," Gran Gran said. "I'm off. Be seeing you." And, with a wink, she vanished.

Winston turned to Megan. "I guess I should start preparing dinner."

She pulled him down, wrapping her arms around his neck. "I'm not really hungry, you know."

Charles Ray

Don't miss the sequel to *Angel on His Shoulder – Revised Edition,* for the further adventures of Winston, Megan, and the irrepressible Gran Gran.

"Do you, Megan Adrianna Berman, take this man, Winston Lee Nesbitt, to have and to hold from this day forward, for better or worse, for richer, for poorer, in sickness and in health, to love and to cherish; from this day forward until death do you part?" The Reverend Vincent Neville's voice picked up by the lapel mike he wore under his dark blue silk suit and transmitted to the speakers positioned along the walls of the cathedral-like Church of Redemption, rang sonorously throughout the room. The room was huge, and made to seem even larger with so few people in it, just the Nesbitt and Berman families, colleagues from Winston and Megan's place of work, and a few of the church officials.

Megan, resplendent in a snow-white gown, her brown face glowing with joy, quivered as she gazed up at the tall, broad-shouldered, brown man standing before her. Her heart pounded, and she wasn't sure it was from happiness at finally getting Winston to propose, or suppressed lust generated by the nearness of a preacher as handsome and sexy as Neville. No, she thought, it's not the preacher; I'm happy to be marrying Winston. Being tall, dark, and handsome is not enough, there has to be a feeling in your heart for a person, and I have feelings for

Winston unlike any I've ever had for another man.

"I do," she said in a quiet voice, and squeezed Winston's arm.

Reverend Neville smiled, his thin lips only slightly parted, revealing gleaming white teeth. He nodded at her and then turned to Winston.

"Do you, Winston Lee Nesbitt, take this woman, Megan Adrianna Berman, to have and to hold from this day forward, for better or worse, for richer, for poorer, in sickness and in health, to love and to cherish; from this day forward until death do you part?"

Winston cleared his throat and looked down at the floor. His stomach felt like it contained a bowling ball and a bottle of seltzer, and he was sweating profusely, and not just because getting married was a new experience; his grandmother was sitting on his shoulder.

Even though he knew that no one but Megan and he could see her; well, one other person sitting in the church could, but Dennis Alexander, the guard from Winston's building, where he and Megan worked as senior analysts for Advantage Consulting, Inc., was accustomed to 'haints' and spirits, and wouldn't let on that he saw the nine-inch, wizened woman perched on the shoulder of Winston's rented tuxedo; Winston was still worried that his grandmother's mischievous spirit would break out and turn the ceremony into pandemonium. She'd done so on more than one occasion since she'd literally popped back into his life on his fortieth birthday, twenty years after she passed away.

"Come on, boy," he heard her cracked voice in his head. *"We ain't got all day. Answer the man."*

At least Winston had mastered the art of conversing with his grandmother in the presence of others.

"Okay, Gran . ., er, granny, I will if you'll just stay out of my mind for a few minutes." He put as much firmness as he could into the thought.

His grandmother sniffed and folded her bony arms across her flat chest. She was wearing a gingham dress that looked like a tiny item of wardrobe from some old western movie, and had her iron-grey hair tied into a bun, making her high-cheeked, light brown face look even more severe than it normally did. The dress, not too unlike what she always wore, was her idea of appropriate dress for the most important day of Winston's life, but she meant well, and he wasn't sure that she had anything else to wear. Even after so long back in his life, he didn't understand how spirits worked. He'd been meaning to ask her, but the occasion had never arisen.

Reverend Neville made a sound in this throat and nodded his head toward Winston, his eyes narrowed; he was accustomed to reluctant grooms, but there was a limit to even his patience.

"Uh, I do," Winston said.

"Thank goodness," Winston heard Megan's voice in his head. *"I was beginning to think maybe you'd changed your mind about marrying me."* She, like him, had the ability to communicate silently, having been able to see Granny from the first, and not at all

being put off at seeing a tiny figure floating in the air or putting words inside her head.

"You know that's not so, Megan, honey. It's just hard for me to concentrate with you and granny popping into my head without warning."

"Sorry," Megan said. *"I'll leave your head alone. You too, Granny; let him have his thoughts to himself."*

"Happy to," Winston's grandmother said. *"He never thinks anything interesting, anyhow. Not like you; thinking 'bout that this long drink of water in front of you."*

Megan blushed. *"Not true! I was not thinking about Reverend Neville."*

"Child, if you wasn't thinking 'bout the good reverend, why you blushing? You best be thinking 'bout how you gonna help Winston Lee here do his duty on your honeymoon. You know he ain't got much experience in that department."

Megan blushed deeper. Winston, who had been an unwilling witness to their mental exchange, blushed as well. He could see how Megan would find the reverend attractive. He was everything Winston wasn't; tall, and slender with a hint of muscle beneath his dark suit, and as the head of one of the most popular churches in northern Virginia, probably rich enough to buy Winston with pocket change.

"Could you two get your minds out of the gutter," he said. *"I'll have you know, I am not as inexperienced as you think. I've had experiences."*

"Your little games in the bathroom when you were a kid don't count," Winston's grandmother said.

Megan put a hand over her mouth to stifle a laugh, while Winston just crossed his eyes in frustration. He'd exaggerated his 'experience.' His one encounter with a woman had been in Texas with some of his buddies from the Air Force, and it had been a disaster.

Reverend Neville, accustomed to strange behavior in couples about to take the serious step into matrimony, ignored their facial by-play, putting it down to nervousness. He cleared his throat, quietly, so that only Winston and Megan could hear. He was an experienced clergyman, and knew how to maintain decorum in his church.

"Inasmuch as marriage is a sacred institution," he said, scowling slightly. "Not to be entered into lightly, but reverently, we come together here today to witness the joining of this couple enter into this holy estate. If any person here can show just cause why they may not be joined together, let them speak now or forever hold their peace."

In the front pew, Winston's mother, who along with his father had come up from Florida for the wedding, started to raise her hand, but his father reached over and clamped it against her thigh, giving her a stern look. She didn't know Megan all that well, and like mothers since time began was miffed that Winston had made such an important decision without consulting her. As for his father, a more pragmatic person, he was just happy that Winston had finally found a woman who would marry him.

Megan's parents, sitting in the front pew across the aisle, looking uncomfortable in

Charles Ray

their stiff clothes, had traveled from South
Carolina, and they merely sat looking
alternately glum and slightly pleased. Her
mother sniffed back tears. Megan had
inherited her mother's looks, round face,
small breasts, and rather chunky thighs, but
she was taller than both of her parents. Her
father was a gaunt looking man with iron-
grey hair that was cropped close to his bullet-
shaped skull. He looked like a country
preacher, and rarely spoke other than
minimal greetings; his wife did the talking for
both, and even she had little to say.

Most of the rest of the congregation sat
quietly in the pews behind Winston's parents.
Dennis Alexander, the guard, beamed
proudly at his friend Winston. Next to him,
his wife Dorrie, a medium brown skinned
woman of broad girth and fierce demeanor,
also sniffed back tears. Co-workers from
Advantage, led by their boss, Leland Carter,
also smiled broadly, but remained silent.

Neville scanned the church, empty except
for the small knot of people. A couple of
Winston's co-workers, the guy from the
mailroom, and the head of custodial services,
were seated behind Megan's parents so that
side of the church wouldn't be empty. Seeing
that no one objected, Neville cleared his
throat.

"Very well, then," he said in his deep
voice. "There being no objections to this
union, by the authority vested in me by the
Commonwealth of Virginia, and before God, I
now pronounce you man and wife. You may
kiss the bride."

After Megan tossed her bridal bouquet,
which was caught by a faded blonde from

accounting, who gushed and showed it to everyone, they retired to a small room off the main cathedral for a lunch that the company had generously paid for.

A large table had been set in the center of the room. In the center of the table, surrounded by a wide assortment of canapés, cold cuts, cheese dips, and little meat sandwiches, was a six-tier wedding cake topped by two figures, a bride and groom, standing under a flowered arch made of little pink blossoms.

Reverend Neville escorted the new couple to the table. He picked up a large knife that had a pink bow tied around the handle.

"Before we partake of this fine repast," he said. "I believe it's customary for you to cut the cake and feed each other a morsel to symbolize your future life of mutual support and love."

He handed the knife to Winston. Grasping the handle together, Winston and Megan cut off a small slice from the bottom tier and slid it onto one of the small plates stacked nearby. Picking up a fork, Winston lifted out a piece of cake and gave it to Megan, smearing a bit of icing on her face. He tried brushing it away, but only succeeded in spreading it wider to the merriment of everyone present.

"Way to go, Winston," one of his co-workers said.

Megan's mother rushed over and, taking a handkerchief from her handbag, wiped the smear away, giving Winston a sour look as she did so. Megan smiled and patted his hand as she took the fork from him. She gave him some cake, smearing icing above his lip.

"Guess you're not the only one a little nervous today," she said as she wiped the smudge away.

Winston knew what she'd done, and was grateful. Everyone else got into the spirit of the party as Megan cut more slices from the cake and served their guests. The food began disappearing at a rapid pace as people descended upon the table, along with the champagne that Winston's father had bought to celebrate his son's wedding.

Megan and Winston were both too nervous, so they ate little. Megan nibbled at some of the chopped carrots and celery, while Winston had a few of the little sausages cooked in pastry. Megan's parents ate sparingly from the vegetable dishes, but Winston noticed that her mother eyed the meat dishes with distaste, and nudged her husband every time he got near one.

Winston's mother came up to the couple and kissed them on the cheek, first Winston, and then Megan.

"I hope the two of you will be happy together," she said.

"Thank you, Mrs. Nesbitt," Megan said. "I know we will."

"This was kind of sudden, wasn't it?" she asked.

"What do you mean, mother?" Winston asked.

"Well, I mean, you never said anything about being engaged even; and not a word about getting married until your father and I got the invitation."

"Megan and I have known each other for a long time," he said. "We've been working

together for years. I'm sorry if we didn't give
you more notice, but you and dad are way
down there in Florida, and I hardly ever hear
from you except on my birthday and at
Christmas."

"But, Winston, you never even told us
you two were dating," she said. "It just came
as a bit of a shock to learn you were getting
married."

The truth was, Winston didn't think his
parents would be interested. He'd visited
them only once since they moved out on him,
and he'd been so bored he'd never gone
again. This was the first time they'd come
back to Washington, too, and they rarely ever
enquired about his activities; just the
inevitable shirt or new pair of pajamas at
Christmas or on his birthday. It hadn't
occurred to him to tell them about Megan.

"Sorry, mom," he said. "I guess it was
kind of sudden. I just didn't think to tell you
about everything I was doing."

"I just want to be sure you're prepared
for the life ahead of you." She turned to
Megan. "And, what about you, young lady;
has anyone talked to you about what it will
be like to be a wife, and hopefully someday, a
mother?"

Megan hadn't had any more contact with
her parents than Winston had with his; but
they seemed unaffected by the suddenness of
her announcement that she was getting
married.

"No, Mrs. Nesbitt," she said. "But, it
can't be all that hard." After all, she thought,
you look like you did it without a lot of
advanced knowledge, although, with all the
quirks Winston had, it hadn't been all that

proficient. "I guess we can learn as we go along."

"I don't know, young lady," Winston's mother said. "It can be complicated, especially after children enter the picture. Learning on the job can be difficult."

"She ought to know," Granny said, floating over to hover in front of Megan. *"She never did learn. No matter what I said to this girl, she just went off and did whatever came into her head."*

"Did she tell you beforehand that she and dad were getting married?" Winston asked.

"Land sakes, no, boy; I didn't find out until after they were already hitched. Ran off and got it done by a justice of the peace. Not that I woulda minded; your daddy's a good man. Frankly, I often thought he was too good for your mother. I know that's not a charitable thing to say about your own daughter, but that girl's always been as empty-headed as they come."

"So, you never got a chance to tell her about things before she got married?" Megan asked.

"Oh, I tried tellin' her the facts of life when she was growing up, but she never listened. Always had a mind of her own; wanting to do everything her own way. Your daddy's too gentle to argue with her, so she pretty much runs things."

Megan wanted most of all for her marriage to Winston to get off on the right foot, so she decided to try and make peace with his mother, who she sensed wasn't completely happy with his choice of a mate.

"Mrs. Nesbitt," she said. "I know there's a lot I need to learn about being a good wife, and someday a good mother. I hope you won't mind if I reach out to you for advice from time to time."

Clearly not expecting this response, Winston's mother took a step back.

"Oh, well, I'm sure you two will be quite happy together, and you seem like a very bright young woman. I don't want to be an intrusive mother-in-law like my own mother was," she said, and then realizing the trap she'd talked herself into, cleared her throat. "But, of course, anytime you have a question, just call me."

"Intrusive? Why you ungrateful little whelp. If I was alive, I'd take you outside and slap you silly," Granny said. *"I never stuck my nose into business that wasn't mine."*

"But, Granny," Winston said. *"I remember when I was little, you were always telling mama she was doing things wrong."*

"Yeah, boy, but that was my business. You were family after all, and she was always doing things wrong."

Other books by this author:

The Buffalo Soldier   series:
Trial by Fire
Homecoming
Incident at Cactus Junction
Renegade
Escort Duty
Battle at Dead Man's Gulch
Peacekeepers
Yosemite
Comanchero
Range War

Al Pennyback mysteries
Color Me Dead
Memorial to the Dead
Deadline
Dead, White, and Blue
A Good Day to Die
The Day the Music Died
Die, Sinner
Deadly Intentions
Death by Design
Till Death Do Us Part
Deadly Dose
Dead Man's Cove
Dead Men Don't Answer
Deadly Paradise
Kiss of Death
Death in White Satin
Death and Taxis
Drop Dead, Gorgeous
Deadbeat
A Deadly Wind Blows

Charles Ray

Other fiction
Angel on His Shoulder
She's No Angel
Child of the Flame
Pip's Revenge
Wallace in Underland
Further Adventures of Wallace in Underland
Dead Letter and Other Tales
The White Dragons
The Dragon's Lair
Dragon Slayer
The Last Gunfighters
The Culling
Frontier Justice: Bass Reeves, Deputy U.S. Marshal
Angel on His Shoulder – Revised Edition

Nonfiction
*Things I Learned from My Grandmother About
  Leadership and Life*
*Taking Charge: Effective Leadership for the Twenty-first
  Century*
Grab the Brass Ring
There's Always a Plan B
*African Places: A Photographic Journey Through
  Zimbabwe and southern Africa*
A Portrait of Africa
In the Line of Fire: American Diplomats in the Trenches

Children's books
The Yak and the Yeti
Samantha and the Bully
Molly Learns to Share

Anthologies and works to which this author has contributed

Inside a U.S. Embassy: Diplomacy at Work (Third Edition)
Awesome Allshorts: Last Days, Lost Ways
Best Poems of 1998
The Drops on the Pine Needles: Education in Shelby County, Texas, 1874-1965
Treasured Poems of America – Summer 1998
Endless Skies of Blue

Charles Ray

About the Author

Charles Ray has been writing fiction since his teens. He won a Sunday school magazine writing contest when he was thirteen, and having his byline on a short story published in a national publication forever hooked him on writing. During his time in the army (1962-1982) he often moonlighted as a newspaper or magazine journalist, and was the editorial cartoonist for the Spring Lake (NC) News, a weekly newspaper, during the 1970s. In addition to his writing, he was an artist/cartoonist and photographer for a number of publications, including Ebony, Eagle and Swan, and Essence, and had a monthly cartoon feature and did several covers for Buffalo, a now-defunct magazine that was dedicated to showcasing the contributions of African-Americans to the country's military history.

After retiring from the army, he joined the U.S. Foreign Service, and served as a diplomat in posts in Asia and Africa until his retirement in 2012. He has worked and traveled throughout the world (Antarctica is the only continent he hasn't visited), and now, as a full time writer, continues to globetrot looking for interesting things to write about, draw, or take pictures of.

A native of Texas, he now calls Maryland

Charles Ray

home. For more on his writing and other projects, check one of the following Web sites:

http://redroom.com/member/charles-a-ray
http://charlesaray.blogspot.com
http://charlieray45.wordpress.com
http://www.twitter.com/charlieray45
http://www.facebook.com/charlieray45
http://www.flickr.com/photos/charlesray45/
http://www.viewbug.com/member/charlesray

If you liked this book, please post a review on Amazon, Goodreads, or your blog to let other readers know.